THE SWORD OF
Denis Anwyck

To order additional copies of *The Sword of Denis Anwyck,*
by Maylan Schurch, call **1-800-765-6955**.

Visit us at **www.reviewandherald.com**
for information on other Review and Herald® products.

THE SWORD OF
DENIS ANWYCK

REVIEW AND HERALD® PUBLISHING ASSOCIATION
Since 1861 | www.reviewandherald.com

The author assumes full responsibility for the accuracy of all facts and quotations as
cited in this book.

This book was
Edited by Gerald Wheeler
Cover design by Trent Truman
Cover art by Joe Van Severen
Typeset: 10.5/12 Sabon

PRINTED IN U.S.A.

13 12 11 10 09   5 4 3 2 1

Library of Congress Cataloging-in-Publication Data

Schurch, Maylan.
  The sword of Denis Anwyck / Maylan Schurch.
      p. cm.
  Summary: Although he is reluctant to train for knighthood, thirteen-year-old Denis
finds that his ability to read and write makes him a key figure in the kingdom when
Baron Mordred mounts a rebellion against the King.
  [1. Knights and knighthood--Fiction. 2. Literacy--Fiction. 3. Adventure and adventur-
ers--Fiction.] I. Title.
  PZ7.S3966Sw 2009
  [Fic]--dc22
                                      2008053722
  ISBN 978-0-8280-2425-9

With love,
to Shelley,
whose honest, blue-eyed sweetness
gives me courage.

With thanks, to Randy Fishell,
who suggested the concept
of this book.

CHAPTER 1

"A," I said.

Magda Judde squinted suspiciously at my thick leather-bound journal that lay open on the table before her. "A?"

"A."

She jabbed a raw red finger at another part of the page. "Then what's that one?"

"That's an O."

"They look the same to me."

Clamping my teeth together to keep from yawning, I slid the book closer to her and pointed. "Look at the little tail on this one. That means it's an A."

"By the way, what does all that say?"

"Those are the king's rules."

Her eyebrows lifted. "You're kidding. Who taught you those?"

"The scholar. Back when I learned to write."

"Anyway," she said briskly, "you say that letter's an O?"

"A."

"Oh."

"It's not an O, Magda. It's an A."

"You know what I meant, Denis Anwyck," she snorted. "And you back there," she said, heaving herself around on her stool and glaring at her son, "that'll be enough out of *you*."

Max had snickered. Almost 14 and a few months older than I was, he was sitting on the floor of the room that served as his father's workshop, attaching a crank to the back of the new crossbow his dad had made him.

"Denis," he said, "come out back with me and see if this works."

"Stay here, Denis," his mother commanded. "I have some spare time right now, and I'm going to make the most of it." She turned back to my journal. "Show me again. Which one is O?"

Life in the Judde house was never dull. When I was 5, my parents dying from the Black Death, the soldiers had come on their horses and found me sobbing as I knelt beside them. Pulling me away kicking and screaming, the men had tied me to a cart. Then plugging their ears to shut out my howling, they had rattled past the king's misty castle high on the hill and brought me to the home of Charles Judde, woodworker.

His wife, Magda, had scooped me up in her arms, the way she scooped up stray dogs and cats and anything else that was homeless, and had made me her son, even though they already had a boy nearly a year older. Charles had beaten me severely the two times I'd tried to run back to my parents' house, but he loves me.

I cannot understand everything that happened back then. In fact, I don't dare think about it too much.

"O, A," Magda repeated, concentrating hard. "Now, write one of them and I'll see if I can tell what it is."

As I flipped through the journal to find a blank page, she watched the handwritten pages flicker past. "Did you write all that?"

"That's right. I write in it every night."

"What do you write?"

"Oh, just things I'm thinking about."

"Private stuff?"

"Yeah." *Private stuff is right,* I thought to myself. *I could be imprisoned for what I've written here, but nobody looks in this book but me. Good thing most people can't read.*

"OK, watch, Magda. I take my quill pen like this, dip it in the ink, and—" I wrote a letter on a clear page.

"That's an A."

"Right. Good eye."

"Give me that." She reached for my pen. "Let me see if I can do it."

Max brightened. "Good. Then Denis and I can go outside." He picked up the crossbow and several arrows.

I glanced at Magda for permission. "Oh, go ahead," she sighed. "And don't worry about your book. I'll be neat with it."

At that instant we heard a clattering outdoors, and a man's voice shouted, "Somebody get the door!"

Max jumped to open it, and his father, Charles, tall and muscular with a cloudy black beard, staggered in carrying a heavy load of rough boards. With a mighty "Hah!" he let the boards fall to the floor.

"Hah!" Charles said again, peering around. He saw Magda at the table writing in my book. "What, no supper yet?"

"Be patient," she mumbled, her brow furrowed in concentration and her tongue protruding from her mouth.

"What are you doing?"

"Nothing against the law, your majesty," she snapped. "If you hadn't kicked up such a fuss five years ago when the king's scholar was teaching Denis, I would have learned to read and write just as well as he can."

Her husband frowned. "You know why I didn't let you study with him."

"You let Denis."

"Denis is not my son." He paused, glancing at me. "Sorry, Denis," he said gruffly. "I didn't mean it like that. But you're—different. You have the right to go your own way, more than the rest of us. Know what I mean?"

My face flushed, but I nodded. "I'm different."

"I love you like a son, and if you want to, you'll be my son forever, but—"

"That's OK. I understand."

"Charles," Magda interrupted, "don't you think it's about time we put the past behind us? I know you didn't agree with the king then—"

"And I don't now."

"—but must you hold a grudge so long? I'm sure he's changed. Don't you remember? The first rule he taught us was 'The king will give you anything you really choose.' I'm sure he wants the best for us. And anyway, that has nothing to do with my wanting to learn letters."

"Yes, it does," he said. "I didn't trust that scholar he sent. The man always had his hood on, tied in front of his chin. You could never really see his face. Who knows what strange ideas that man had? Those king's rules, for one thing."

"Charles—" Magda began.

Charles assumed a falsetto voice. " 'Be fearlessly honest with your king and yourself,' " he quoted. "Hah! Why does he say that when he doesn't mean it? Just let any of us try to be fearlessly honest with him. He'd have us in the castle dungeon before we knew what hit us."

Max, behind his father's back, beckoned to me and began tiptoeing to the door, crossbow and arrows in hand.

"Well," Magda said, "since one of the rules says 'Record and remember the past,' it's not surprising that the king sent a scholar to—"

Charles interrupted her. "I think the scholar's job was to put a sugarcoating over all the rotten things the king has done."

"Charles, be careful. The boys . . ."

"They need to know the truth, Magda."

"I wish the baron could be king," Max said.

Charles ran to him and took him by the throat. "Too far, my boy, too far!" he shouted. "We speak our minds in this house, but we do not speak treason. If I hear that you have spoken this outside our roof, I will beat you. Do you understand?"

"Yes," Max whimpered.

"Max," his father threatened, "if the king catches wind of what you have said, he will throw us all into the castle dungeon."

"You don't know that, Charles," Magda protested.

"I hate him!" I said suddenly. I didn't plan to say it—it just came out. "I hate the king!"

Charles turned on me, his face purple. "And you!" he roared. "You may be a little lost-dog orphan, but you're under my roof, and you'll protect this household if I have to—"

"I hate him," I cried. "I hate the king! His soldiers came and—"

A shadow fell on the room. Someone stood in the open doorway. His face gray with fear, Charles turned to face the newcomer.

CHAPTER 2

A girl about my own age stood in the entrance to the shop. Her straight hair was a deep gold and her eyes a dark blue. I'd never seen her before in my life.

"Master Judde?" she said in a low, clear voice.

"Yes?" Charles cleared his throat. "How can I be of assistance?"

"I'm here to pick up a wooden chest for the baron's wife."

"Oh, the chest." His manner relaxed and became respectful as he crossed the shop. "Why, certainly. Let's see. Yes, we did finish that a day or two ago . . . and here it is right over here." He picked up a beautifully carved box and glanced doubtfully at the girl. "You'll be taking it with you?"

"Yes. The baroness asked me to."

"Perhaps the baroness did not realize how heavy it might be. You have no carriage?"

"No, but it isn't too far. It's just a half mile to her town house."

"Still, that is not very close. Denis, why don't you carry this for the girl?"

Nodding, I hurried to the table. Magda had arisen too, out of respect for someone connected with the baroness, and had left my writing utensils where they were. Quickly

I stoppered the ink bottle, wiped the pen with a little rag, closed the book, and slid everything into my leather backpack. Then lacing it shut, I slung it between my shoulders by its single strap.

"Thank you for carrying the chest," the girl said when we had reached the street.

"No problem. It might have been a bit heavy for you."

"Will you be able to handle it all right?"

"Sure."

After that we walked in silence for a while. Hugging the box to my chest, I stayed a little behind her, partly out of courtesy, and partly because from that position I could get a better look at her. I felt embarrassed because I didn't know what rank she was and what to call her.

She couldn't have been merely a servant. Her long dress, though simple in design, was a delicate blue, and her back was as straight as an arrow, as though she rode horses.

Just then she turned her head to smile at me. "Your name is Denis?"

"Yes."

"Your father is a good workman."

I looked shyly down at the lid of the chest. "He's not my father. I'm adopted."

She walked on in silence, probably waiting to see if I'd say more. But it was so deep and painful a story that I didn't know if I could tell it right and still seem like a normal person. So I kept quiet.

We now walked beside a dark-green meadow bounded on three sides by tall trees. In the meadow grazed a giant white mare. As we approached, the horse immediately lifted her head and looked at us.

Although I wanted to ask the girl if she rode horses, I still felt tongue-tied. If she were living in the baron's town house, who was she? I knew the baron didn't have a daughter. From the way she dressed and spoke I knew that she wasn't a servant. She must be a relative, and therefore she must be a noble, and as a commoner I had no right to ask personal questions. But I did need something to talk about.

Then I saw the twig.

Beside the meadow a farmer had strung a long rope between two buildings, probably to cure animal hides on.

Near one end of the line a Y-shaped twig was hanging upside down, caught by its crotch.

"Look at that," I said, pointing.

She paused. "Where?"

"That twig. Like an upside-down Y. I guess the wind last night must have blown it up there."

The girl stared at it. "It's funny it didn't blow back down again."

"The two branches of the Y-fork are too heavy," I explained. "As long as the twig rests its full weight on the line, nothing can move it."

As we resumed our walk, she lapsed into silence for a time. Then when we turned into the street where the baron's town house stood, she suddenly stopped and turned to me.

"You said the twig was like a Y. Do you know letters?"

I watched her, wondering whether I should tell her. Finally I said, "Yeah. I can read and write."

"I saw you putting something that looked like a big book into your backpack. Do you always carry it with you?"

"Yeah. I don't want anyone to steal it."

"That's a beautiful backpack."

"Thanks. I triple-stitched it and rubbed it with oil to keep the water out."

"You made it yourself?" New respect showed in her eyes. "Do you mind if I ask you how you learned to write?"

Though I paused again, somehow I felt more confident now. I still didn't know who she was, but she seemed to treat me as her equal.

"When I was 8," I said, "the king sent a scholar down to the village every Thursday morning. He went from door to door saying that he was starting a school, and he told parents if they wanted their children to learn to read and write, they could send them to him."

"Wow! How many children were there in the school?"

"I was the only one."

Her eyes opened wide. "The only one?"

I nodded. "In fact, after a while I was his only student, period. There were two or three adults for a while, but they lost interest. And parents didn't want their children to go to school."

"Why not?"

We had stopped outside the baron's magnificent three-story house. "Well, it's hard to explain. A lot of them had bad feelings about the king. They still do. And when they found out that it was the king who had sent the scholar . . ."

"Why did they have bad feelings?"

I glanced sideways at her face. If I just knew who she was, I could decide how freely to speak. "It was just after the Black Death," I said carefully. "The king's soldiers were very brutal. They seemed to have no pity."

"No pity?"

"None." Suddenly I felt angry, and it made me reckless.

"My parents were both dying. I was their only child. I was with them beside their bed. Father was very quiet. Maybe he was already dead. I was holding on to my mother's hand. She had lost her mind then, and was saying strange things, but she said very clearly, over and over, that she loved me."

The girl reached out and put her hand on my arm. When I looked down at my hand and saw that it was trembling, I snatched it away from her.

"Don't tell me any more if you don't want to," she said softly.

"And then the soldiers came," I continued. "A knight and six or seven armed villeins. They crashed their way through the door and stood looking at us. My mother stared at them with her eyes open, wide, and screamed, and drew me to her."

I turned my head away.

"And then I heard the knight say, 'Get him.' And they grabbed me away from her. She had hold of my sleeve, and it tore. Then she screamed at them again, and tried to hit them, but they picked me up and carried me out. I kicked one of them in the throat. I could hear her calling my name from inside the house. I broke loose and ran back toward the door, but they caught me again and tied me to a cart."

Then I turned and looked the girl full in the face. What I saw filled me with wonder. The sun shone brightly on a wide tear-track down her left cheek. But she didn't say anything. And she didn't wipe away the tear. So I said, "May I know your name?"

"Alinor. Alinor . . . Artois."

Ice filled my lungs. "Artois," I repeated faintly. "That's the king's family name."

After glancing in each direction, she looked back into my eyes. "You've told me your secret," she said. "I'll tell you mine. Other people know me as Alinor Dagworth, even the baroness. But I am Lady Alinor Artois, the king's grand-daughter. I am next in line to the throne."

CHAPTER 3

Immediately I sank to one knee. "Forgive me, Your Lady-ship, for—"

"Get up, get up," she hissed, grasping my arm in a surprisingly strong grip and hauling me to my feet. "Laugh! Quickly!"

I stared at her.

"Laugh. Pretend you were making fun of me."

With a forced smile I managed the fakiest laugh I've ever given. "Ha, ha, ha, ha."

Laughing more believably, she reached down and scooped up a handful of gravel and flung it at me. "Throw some at me," she said.

I pretended to do the same.

Then she came close. "What is your name?"

"Denis Anwyck, My Lady."

"Don't call me 'My Lady.' Never do that again. Call me Alinor. I can't explain right now, but it is very important." Her voice became low and steady. "You must keep my secret if we are to be friends."

"Friends?"

"It is vital that people not know who I am. The baroness thinks I'm Alinor Dagworth, a noble girl here for the summer. She doesn't even know the king ever had a grand-daughter. No one must suspect."

"Why?"

She looked doubtfully at me. "I don't think I'll tell you that yet." Suddenly she glanced back at the house. "But I've got to go. Here. Give me the chest. Thanks for helping me." As she reached out to take the chest from me, her cool fingers brushed mine. And then she disappeared into the house.

As I walked back home, I thought, *She's 13 too. Or close to it. But can I trust her? Did I say too much? If she's really the king's granddaughter, why is she next in line for the throne? That sounds suspicious. Wouldn't her father be heir? What will happen if she tells the king what I said? Will the knights come for me again? I've heard stories about the cruelty—*

Then I grinned self-consciously. *Who do I think I am, anyway? What would the king care about an orphan rat like me? Who knows what the king thinks, anyway?*

And who cares?

"Record and remember the past." Well, if that's what he wants, I've got it all recorded in my book. But one thing's for sure—he wouldn't like a lot of what I've written.

On the way home I mulled over in my head some other things I'd write in my book tonight in that wonderful secret code, the alphabet.

As I passed the mare in the meadow (she looked up again), I noticed the twig still swinging back and forth on the rope line.

My hand was on the leather doorstrap of the Juddes' front door, ready to pull it open, when the wood exploded in front of my face. Splinters flicked my cheeks, and one even got in my eye. Blinking rapidly through rivers of tears, I knelt, trying to remove the splinter.

"Denis?" A faint, high voice spoke in my ear. "Denis? Are you OK?"

"Max, you idiot!" I yelled. "Was that your crossbow?"

"Yeah." His voice lowered an octave and got more confident. "Are you all right? I didn't get your eye, did I?"

"There's a splinter in it."

"Here, let me look."

"No . . . there. I think it's gone." My vision began to improve. When I could see Max clearly, I glared at him.

"What did you think you were trying to do, anyway?"

"I wanted to scare you. But I guess I haven't got the hang of aiming it yet. Sorry."

"Forget it. Just don't use my nose for target practice anymore. Let me see the crossbow."

"Here." He handed it to me. "Come around back and try it out."

We went behind the house. "Max, are you sure you're supposed to have one of these?"

"What are you talking about?"

"Isn't there some sort of law that bans these for commoners?"

"Oh, this is just a kid's toy. The bowpiece is too weak for actual combat. Dad made sure of that."

"I know, but the way that bolt slammed into the door in front of me—this isn't a kid's toy."

Max chuckled. "Crank it up and try it yourself."

A full-strength crossbow's string has a lot of tension on it, and you can't pull it back with your fingers the way you can a longbow's. You have to actually crank it back, far enough so that the string goes over the notch in the nut. Then you take off the crank, put your bolt, or arrow, on the bow, aim it, and pull the iron trigger underneath. And anybody downrange from your bolt who isn't protected by a quarter inch of armor plate is a goner. Even chain mail won't stop a full size crossbow.

Max's string was too hard to pull by hand, so I placed the crossbow nose down into the dirt, cranked it, nutted the string, and raised it to my shoulder.

"Not so fast," Max interrupted. "You forgot the bolt. There." He notched a thick, feathered arrow into place. "Watch out. The trigger's touchy."

I strolled through the back yard to a reed-lined swampy area. A whistle high in the large tree on the swamp's edge caused me to look up. There, about 15 feet above me, perched a blackbird with a red patch on its wing.

Raising the crossbow, I took aim, sighting right along the top of the bolt directly at the red splash on his wing. Slowly I tightened my finger on the trigger.

Whaaackk!

The bowstring hummed tautly, and leaves from the tree drifted down into the swamp.

Max was chortling with glee. "You got him, Denis! You got him!"

I blinked. "Where is he?"

"Down below, down there in the reeds. I didn't see a lot of feathers fly, but he dropped like a stone! Good shot!"

A slow grin spread across my face as I hefted the crossbow in my hands. This was fun. Maybe I could cajole Charles into making me one of my own.

Then I heard the thrashing in the reeds. The bird. It wasn't dead. I'd merely wounded it, and now it was down there going through its death struggle. I could hear it flopping horribly in the water, drowning by inches.

Flinging the crossbow aside, I lunged into the reeds.

"Denis, what're you doing?"

"Max, help me! Help me find that bird. We've got to put it out of its misery."

"You idiot, let it die! You'll get yourself wet."

Still, I searched through the reeds. The water was up to my knees, and it seemed to be deeper farther out. Somewhere among the cattails the bird was still beating its wings in its death struggle.

CHAPTER 4

I never found the redwing. The reeds were too thick and the water too deep, and I didn't want my backpack to get wet. So finally I turned and struggled back to shore and ran, sobbing, to a corner of the yard that was as far away as possible from the swamp.

Max followed me.

"Denis, Denis," he kept saying in a voice that blended amazement, scorn, and pity. "What's wrong with you? It was only a stupid little bird. What are you, a girl or something?"

Unable to answer, I kept crying.

"Listen," he said, shaking me savagely. "Is this how a knight would behave? Think of the baron. Would the baron start blubbering because he shot a bird? You're a coward, Denis."

I slugged him in the stomach, and he punched me back.

"Tell you what, Denis," he said when I at last managed to get more control of myself. "You don't say anything about this, and I won't. OK?"

I cleared my throat a couple of times to get the quaver out. "OK."

"Promise?"

"Promise."

"Because," he continued, "if word got around about this,

the other kids would think you were weirder than ever."

"What do you mean, weirder than ever?"

Max slapped my backpack. "This leather bag you carry on your back all the time. It makes you look like a peddler. I feel like a fool walking around with you when you're wearing it. It would be one thing if you carried a dagger in it, or something sensible. But no, all you've got is that writing stuff."

I glared at him through bleary eyes. "Lay off me. You play with your toys, and I'll play with mine. OK?"

His mouth became a thin, narrow line.

"You are out of it, buddy," he said. "Just out of it, that's all. I'm telling you these things for your own good. The other kids think you're off your head. They think you aren't normal."

"Lay off me, Max. The king's rules say to record and remember the past, and to be fearlessly honest with your king and yourself. That's what I'm doing in this book. Only," I said grimly, "I'm not sure the king would like what I'm being fearlessly honest about."

Max scowled at me. "If you don't watch it, Denis, people are going to think you're nuts. Nobody'll hire you when you have to go to work. My dad's not going to let you sponge off us forever."

"Shut up. I never asked your dad for anything."

"Then why don't you just walk out of here? Right now. Why don't you just—"

"Max!" came a bellow from the back door. "Where are you?"

"Here, Dad," Max called. He stared at me for one second more. "Just remember what I say. And shape up. I know you're a poor little orphan and all that, and we're supposed to pity you, but get with it. If you don't, you'll get left behind. OK?"

When I didn't say anything, he turned to go, then came back again. "Oh, by the way," he said in a calmer voice. "I'm getting some guys together for a play-joust tomorrow morning out in Loring Meadow. Be there."

"Maybe I will, maybe I won't."

Max scratched his chin and looked at me thoughtfully. "Well, at least you've got guts. And a mouth."

That night I wrote a lot. About the bird and Alinor and everything.

I did go to the joust the next day, just to see Max's latest crazy scheme. A lot of boys my age had gathered in Loring Meadow (the same one where I'd seen the white horse and the twig). A whole bunch of younger kids were there too, standing off to the side watching.

My interest perked up when I saw the quintain. All the boys had clustered around it. It was a thick wooden post about six feet high, nailed to a flat platform that rested on the meadow grass. A small barrel had been upended over the top of the post.

On the front of the barrel someone had nailed a wooden board about two feet square, with a bull's-eye painted in the center and a wooden pole placed horizontally across the top of the target. Tied to one end of the pole was a rope, and to the rope a stone about the size of my fist.

Max seemed to have put himself in charge. "Line up, line up, line up," he kept shouting. "I'll go first and show you how to do it. But you've got to line up."

The other boys formed a ragged line. I stood at the end

of it—not that I really wanted to take part, but I didn't want them to consider me one of the littler boys, who were watching us enviously from farther away.

"OK," Max said, "here's my lance, right?" He raised a six-foot shaft in his right fist. "And this is my shield." Strapped to his left arm with a leather thong was a wide piece of tree bark.

"Now watch." He ran toward the quintain, holding his lance point before him. The point struck off-center on the target. This made the pole swing the rock around. Just before the rock could hit his back, Max held up his shield, and the stone bounced off. You could tell he'd had a lot of practice.

"See? If you hit the target in the middle, the whole quintain topples over. If you miss, like I did, the pole swings the stone around, and you've got to be quick with your shield or you'll get conked. Got it?"

Several doubtful murmurs came from the other boys.

"OK. Who's next? Edward, you're next in line. Here's the lance and shield. Go!"

Edward missed the target entirely, and bumped the quintain with his shoulder. He loped to the rear of the line to stand behind me amid lots of laughter.

"Ralph!" Max shouted.

Although Ralph hit the target, it was not in the exact center. He had been concentrating so hard on the target that the rock came as a surprise, giving him a severe thump just below the back of his neck. Several boys insisted that we use a smaller rock, but Max refused.

And so they went down the line, each watching the others carefully, some of them stepping out of line to rehearse the movements. Once in a while a boy would charge too cautiously, afraid of the swinging rock, and Max would always scream at him to do it again. "Even if you miss," he yelled, "if you're fast enough you'll go right by, and the rock will miss you!"

And finally it was my turn.

"Denis!"

Gripping the lance, I cradled it tightly against my right rib cage, and brought the shield up near my left cheekbone. Then focusing on the circle, I took a breath and was about to charge when somebody (Ralph, I think) shouted, "Hey! He's wearing the backpack! No fair!"

I turned around. "What's it to you?"

"That's cheating!" Ralph insisted. "He's got to take off his backpack. If the rock hits him, he won't even feel it."

"Get your own backpack," I said.

Max walked up to me. "Take it off, Denis."

"No."

"This is a knightly tournament, and knights are honorable. They give themselves no unfair advantage. Take it off."

"I never take this backpack off when I'm outside the house. You know that."

Leaning close to me, Max hissed under his breath, "Denis, I am about this far from knocking you off your feet. Are you my friend or aren't you?" His voice rose to an audible command. "Get your backpack off."

The others crowded around. I could see the demon light of fun in their eyes. Some circled behind me. I felt a tug, and then another.

Gripping the strap tightly, I snapped, "Let me alone."

"Come on, orphan rat," Ralph said.

"Keep your hands off that pack!" I yelled. "Somebody else can have the lance. Just leave me alone!"

It was the wrong thing to say, of course. In an instant they leaped upon me. Ducking to my knees, I twisted over, trying to lie on my backpack to protect its precious contents.

But they were too quick. As several boys held my hands, I saw the glint of a knife and watched it descend to the strap, its blade straining against the leather.

CHAPTER 5

"Look!" screamed someone above me. "The king is out riding! He's coming this way!" In an instant, amid the vanishing thunder of feet, I found myself alone.

"Thank you, Your Majesty," I whispered, rolling over on my side and checking my backpack strap to make sure it was undamaged. Over by the road all the boys—older and younger ones alike—stood in a perfectly straight line, looking to the left.

I hurried to join them.

Stepping out into the road, Max shaded his eyes. "I thought somebody said the king was coming. I can't see him."

"He's behind those trees now," one of the boys replied.

"Do you guys all know what to do?" Max asked anxiously. "When his horse gets within 10 paces, you go to your knees. And then when he—"

"Knock it off, Max," a boy said. "We know all that."

Suddenly Max's face lit up. "Wait!" he shouted. "Let's go back and practice with the quintain. Let's pretend we don't see him until he's real close. Then we'll all rush over here and kneel. That way he'll see us practicing to become knights, and maybe—"

"Yeah! Yeah! Let's go!" Caught up in the idea, the older

boys instantly lined up to face the target. Since I still held the lance and shield, Max took them from me. The knowledge that His Majesty's eye might even now be upon him caused him to charge the target with extra speed. *Clunk.* The quintain toppled.

Immediately the next boy took the lance. Although he too lunged viciously at the target, he missed. The stone whirled and bobbed madly on the end of the rope, striking him on the side of the head, but though pale, he staggered back to his place.

The fifth boy had just taken the lance when Max shouted, "His Majesty approaches! Bow the knee!"

Everyone rushed to the road and knelt. Three riders approached, the king astride the center horse, a powerful stallion. The two other riders were knights that I recognized, though none wore armor, not even chain mail. And not even swords.

The king was bareheaded, his shoulder-length hair a beautiful silver. His face was nut-brown above his beard. He looked down on us with interest.

Suddenly Max arose from his knees and stepped out into the road. "Your Majesty," he cried, "accept the worship of your worthy knights." And he knelt again, directly in front of the king's horse.

The two knights with the king tried to conceal grins behind their mustaches. One of them raised his hand as though he were about to gesture the boys away, when the king said, "Pause a moment, Sir Eric."

The two men immediately reined their horses back a few paces.

"Rise, gentlemen," the king said to us. Our knees trembling, we rose. In one breathtakingly smooth motion he dismounted, tossed the reins up to Sir Eric, and walked over to where we stood shivering with excitement. Never before had we seen our king so close to us. I looked intently at his brown, wrinkled face, and at his eyes. They were a deep, dark blue and very alive. For an instant his gaze flickered over my face, and I felt its power.

Then he glanced over our heads to the jousting field. "So you set up a quintain, did you?"

"Yes, Your Majesty," Max said respectfully, but his voice was bursting with pride that the king had noticed. "Your Majesty's worthy knights were practicing to fight your future battles."

Come on, Max, I thought to myself. *We're in the presence of royalty, and you have to shoot off your mouth.*

"Very brave of you," the king replied absently. "May I know your names? You, sir," he said to one of the younger boys. "What may I call you?"

"Lionel."

"'Your Majesty,'" Max hissed in the boy's ear.

"Li-Lionel, Your Majesty," the child quavered.

"Where do you live, Lionel?"

"Back there in the village, Your Majesty," he pointed.

"And you, sir. Your name?"

Down the line His Majesty went, asking the names of each boy and who their parents were, then inquiring about their favorite games and what they wanted to do when they grew up. As I watched, I marveled. The whole experience was more like a visit from someone's grandfather than an audience with the king of the nation.

"And you, sir, my valiant young knight," the king turned

to Max. Was my hearing bad, or was there a touch of mockery in His Majesty's tone? "By which name may I address you?"

"My name is Max, Most Noble Sire," said my friend, who had evidently been privately rehearsing this moment, "and my greatest wish is to receive the buffet of knighthood from Your Majesty's sword."

The king's silver eyebrows rose. Then a smile quirked a corner of his mouth. "You are aware, are you not, that under the customs of the time villeins are almost never knighted?"

"There is precedent, Sire," Max answered in a flash. "Sir Bertrand du Guesclin, some years back. He was a villein, but his valiant battles on behalf of his king caused him to be given the buffet."

"You are well up on your military history," the king commented quietly.

He turned to me. "And you, young man. What is your name?"

"Denis, Your Majesty."

"And the names of your parents?"

My eyes dropped. "I have no parents, Sire." Two or three boys giggled nervously.

"The Black Death?" he asked gently.

"Yes, Sire."

"I am sorry." And he laid a giant hand upon my shoulder. And as he did so, the ground swirled beneath me and a memory flickered at the edge of my consciousness—but disappeared.

Max's unpleasant voice brought me back to reality. "His Majesty asked you a question, Denis. Answer it."

My face reddened. "Please, Sire, my mind was elsewhere for a moment."

"May I ask what you carry in your backpack?" the king repeated. Out of the corner of my eye I could see the other boys looking at each other. None dared snicker, but I knew what they were thinking. I swallowed.

"I have learned to write, Sire, and I carry about with me a large book, and a pen, and some ink."

The king studied me intently. "You can write? May I see your book?"

Hurriedly I slipped off my backpack, unlaced the flap, and pulled out the leatherbound journal. Opening it to a page displaying my best penmanship, I handed it to him.

"What do you write in your book?"

I flushed. It was unusual for someone to take such an interest in my hobby, and I didn't know how to handle it. "Just the events of the day, Sire, and my own thoughts."

"Excellent. It is always good to record and remember the past. Don't stop your writing. And above all, write what you really believe." He closed the book and gave it back. "Young men, I must be leaving. May you be at peace. Sir Eric, my horse!" And before any of us had wakened from the dream, the three horsemen had vanished in a cloud of dust.

Max broke the spell—as he always does. " 'May you be at peace,' " he murmured contemptuously in a voice so soft that only I heard it.

CHAPTER 6

To my great surprise, Alinor knocked on the Juddes' door early the next day. "I need your help," she said when I went to see who was there. "Rather quickly. Can you come to the castle right away?"

I stared at her. "Me? The castle?"

"Yes."

"Why?"

"You're needed there. I'll tell you on the way." I strapped on my backpack, and we walked quickly down the road. "We must hurry. You really can write?"

"Sure."

"Good. Sir Robert, my grandfather's prime minister, needs an important letter written."

"Why can't he write it?"

She grinned. "Almost none of the nobles know how. That's what they hire scribes for."

"And there's no scribe at the castle?"

"He's quite sick. Grandpa knows how to write, but he's out riding."

"I met His Majesty yesterday," I said, and told her about the jousting incident.

"Ohhhh," she said, as if I had just solved a great mystery. "That explains why Sir Robert was so anxious for me to bring you. Grandpa probably told him about your penmanship."

When we reached the castle, instead of leading me across the open drawbridge, Alinor guided me to the base of the huge wall. "How do we get in if we don't use the drawbridge?" I asked.

"Remember, we're just kids on a walk," she replied. "The people inside the castle know me, but if outsiders saw me walking across the drawbridge, they'd think it suspicious that a commoner would be so brave. There's a secret entrance."

"I didn't know this castle had a secret entrance."

"Actually, it's more like a secret exit. Most castles have them. Some even have tunnels under the moat itself."

"Why?"

"In case for some reason you want to get out of the castle without anyone noticing."

Slipping behind a small bush, she tugged at one of the wall blocks. It moved and swung back, revealing that it was flat like a door. The dark opening of a passageway appeared in the wall. Alinor bent down and entered, and I followed. After she swung the stone door shut, we ascended a short flight of stairs that led up into the courtyard itself.

As we crossed the sunlit courtyard, a strange feeling came over me. *This castle doesn't seem like a king's residence,* I told myself.

Old war engines slept in corners, surrounded by bales of hay. An immense stone catapult had a young milk cow chewing thoughtfully on its rotted rope strands. Three giant crossbows, mounted on tripods, were gray and cracked with age.

"Wait here," Alinor said. "I'll see if Sir Robert is ready." She returned in a moment. "He's still thinking of what he wants to say. Let me give you a quick tour of the castle."

We circled the huge courtyard in the shadow of the outer walls, then peered into the stables. Stable hands bowed and smiled at Alinor, and glanced at me in surprise.

While we explored, Alinor told me why she was concealing her identity. "Grandpa brought me home from the country where my parents had moved. He wants me to live among the people in the village. That's what he'd like to do himself. In fact, he's planning to someday."

"I thought kings are supposed to live in castles."

"Grandpa doesn't think so. He thinks castles are stupid. He says that the only reason for a castle is to keep out enemies, and he doesn't want any enemies." She looked around thoughtfully. "One of these days he's going to tear this one down."

I blinked. "That's one of his rules, isn't it?"

"Right. 'Tear down your castle.' He thinks his puts up too much of a barrier between him and the people."

"You say he sent you to live in the village?"

"Right. So I can get practice being with ordinary people."

"Like me."

She looked at me and grinned. "You're not ordinary."

Just then we entered the "keep," the large central building. As we climbed the tower staircase, servants bowed and curtseyed to us, giving me mild questioning looks. Ascending past the guard room and the Great Hall, we finally arrived at the royal chambers beneath the top turrets. There we crawled out a window and onto a narrow little bridgeway that arched over the courtyard, connecting the keep to the top of the outer castle walls. Alinor dashed gracefully across it.

"Come on," she called back. "Don't look down and you'll be all right."

Cautiously I stepped across the bridge, and soon we stood in one of the corner watchtowers on the wall itself. Down below I saw the town, and farther out, the whole countryside—even the baron's gray castle five miles away. The two us stood there for some time. Finally Alinor broke the silence. "Sir Robert's probably ready now. We'd better go see him."

We met him as he came up a lower staircase. He was a short, bald man with a beard and a cheerful voice. "Thank you for coming, Denis," he greeted me. "I'm glad to see that the king's scholar had at least one faithful student. His Majesty tells me you write well."

"I enjoy writing, Sir Robert."

"Excellent. Let's go to the Great Hall."

Alinor disappeared in the direction of her chambers, and I followed Sir Robert up to the Great Hall. The knight seated me at a table and gave me a new quill pen, then began to dictate his letter. I wrote what he said on a large sheet of smooth oriental paper.

The message was a long and boring one. Apparently two barons in another kingdom were at war with each other, and one of them was seeking our king's help. Sir Robert was giving the king's decision: our country was neutral, we had always been neutral, and we did not wish to be involved in the fighting.

"And that's that," said Sir Robert with satisfaction once

I'd written the final sentence. "Thank you for your help. I hope we may meet again." Picking up the letter, he hurried off, waving it in the air to dry the ink.

Surprised at being left alone so quickly, I began to wander around the Great Hall. The tapestries I didn't pay much attention to. They were pictures of farm scenes and villages and once in a while a battle. Over at one end of the room stood a giant wooden cupboard twice as tall as I was. Beside the cupboard was something that did catch my attention. It was a tall, narrow pulpit or reading stand. On top of it lay a giant leatherbound book with thick covers.

I don't get to see books very often. When I do, they draw me like a magnet. Carefully I lifted the heavy cover. On the first page someone with beautiful handwriting had written the king's seven rules. I knew them well. They were the first sentences the scholar had taught me to write:

1. The king will give you anything you really choose.
2. Be fearlessly honest with your king and yourself.
3. Record and remember the past.
4. Respect those who give you life.
5. Treat people as though they mean well.
6. Go to the mountain before you answer; go again before you act.
7. Tear down your castle.

The next page contained only a title: *The Chronicles of Pestilence, Being an Account of the Dread Black Death and Times Following.*

Turning another page, I began to read. How long I stood there, absorbed in the book, I don't know, but suddenly I heard distant shouting and calling. Thumping sounded in the corridor outside, and a man's voice said, "Hurry! Prepare the Great Hall! The baron is here!"

"Has the king returned?" a woman asked.

"Yes, he's just come back. But no one was expecting the baron. Hurry!"

Seeing no way to escape, I darted in terror behind the tall cupboard and crouched there, hoping no one would notice me.

CHAPTER

My heart thumping, I waited, hearing the rapid scratching of a broom and of a table being moved. And then silence.

I was about to peer cautiously out from behind the cupboard when there came the sound of two sets of jingling footsteps. Spurs. Only knights or royalty wore spurs. And another sound that caused my heart to leap against my ribs: rapid panting and the scratch of claws on the wooden floor.

I must not move, I told myself. *Nor must I sweat. Dogs can smell sweat.*

The scraping of claws approached until I could see the dog, a glossy black hunter. He was sniffing the corners, the tapestries, the doorways.

"This," the voice of the king said, "is an unexpected pleasure, Mordred."

"Is it really, Your Majesty?" The baron's voice was deep with a harsh edge to it.

Silence. The dog had stopped sniffing and was now slowly turning in a circle, maybe 20 feet from where I stood, preparing to find a place to doze.

"Of course it is a pleasure, my boy. Why, you were once my squire, and then my knight. Every time I see you I think of those good days together."

"It is not the past that I have come to see you about, Sire," the baron replied heavily. "It is the future."

"The future?"

"Yes. The future you are denying your country."

The dog, now lying on the floor, began to growl under its breath.

"Garth! Quiet!" the baron snapped. "Your Majesty, if you will not see things my way, there is no future."

"There is always future, Mordred."

"Let me make myself clearer. There is no future for your kingdom."

"You mean, no future for me."

The jingle of spurred feet sounded on the floor. The baron must have risen and begun pacing back and forth, because his voice now began to change position.

"Sire, I insist that you allow me to take my knights to support the Baron de Milagro in his war against Costello."

"I forbid it. Sir Robert has just dispatched a letter to Milagro saying that I wish to remain neutral in this conflict."

There sounded a heavy thump, as though a fist had descended on a table. The baron roared, "Why did you not consult me first?"

"Why should I consult you?" the king asked mildly. "I knew your answer to start with. You are always in favor of war."

The dog Garth, aroused by the crash of the fist, lifted his head and began sniffing again.

"Are we alone?" the baron demanded tensely.

"Certainly."

"Garth is behaving strangely. If your spies are listening to us—"

"Mordred, Mordred," the king sighed. "After all the years you spent in this castle, can't you trust me? If I wished, I could have you placed in irons and thrown into the dungeon at the bottom of the keep. But you know I don't work that way."

The baron laughed. "You wouldn't dare."

"Daring has nothing to do with it."

"You wouldn't dare because the majority of the country is on my side."

"That is not true."

"You are out of touch with your subjects."

"I am not out of touch. I go riding every day to speak with them."

"Yet they fear you, Sire. They repeat stories of how you treated them in the time of the plague. They complain because you have no desire to extend your land through honorable battle. They despise you because our country is not in tune with the times. They are puzzled by your rules. They do serve you not from love but from fear. And they regard you as a coward."

"Do you regard me as a coward, Mordred?"

The baron did not answer.

"I'll join swords with you this moment," the king said calmly. "*En garde?* "

Another pause. Then the baron laughed. "I would not spoil your beautiful tapestries with your blood, Your Majesty. I simply wish to inform you of something you have not yet grasped: your people long to enjoy the same privileges, and the same knightly glory, as other nations. In my own castle I have 15 knights who have not seen action in seven years. What use is it to train squires? They're not needed in this dismally calm land."

"And people live quietly and prosperously in the villages," the king added, "and no one needs stand atop my castle towers watching for bandits. We are at peace, and peace is good."

"We are getting flabby," the younger man snapped. "If my knights have no practice in battle, they'll be unprepared when they do have to face it."

"And battle will not come unless you bring it. Mountains guard our country on three sides and the river on the south. We can live happily in peace for 200 years to come."

"Your Majesty, one of your rules states that you will give us anything we really desire."

"That is true."

"What if I desired your kingdom?"

"The choice would not be yours alone."

"Others feel the same way."

"I know otherwise," the king replied mildly. "I have many who support me and believe in me."

"Your Majesty, we have talked too long. I demand action. Either you allow us to enter the fray on the side of Milagro, or I go to the people."

"Mordred—"

"I will tell you what I will do. Who cares if your spies hear? First I will stop paying your grain tax. The people will hear about it. Then I will command all knights and villeins in my barony to recant their oath of fealty to you. Naturally you will come to besiege my castle, but because I have made it much stronger than yours, you will not be able to capture it. Even if you did, you would find no one but women and children there—because I and my knights and villeins will have gone to join the war against Costello."

A rustling sounded. Apparently the baron had arisen.

"And when my knights return, hot and hardened from battle, who knows what will happen then?"

"I know what will happen," the king answered. "We'll rejoin the rest of the pitiful, battle-scarred, plague-blasted continent."

"Worse than that will happen," the baron said flatly. "The country may decide that your rule must end."

"That is not the worst that can happen."

"What do you mean?"

"You yourself may wish to take the kingdom."

Silence. The dog slept.

"I must go," the baron said finally. "I desire an answer from you the week after the fair, and certainly by Royal Day. Remember what I have said."

"I will remember far better than you remembered the careful training I gave you, Mordred."

Spurs jingled on the floor. The dog awoke, alert. Turning his shiny black head, he saw me, and his hackles rose. Slowly he rose to his feet, growling.

"Garth!" called the baron. "Heel!"

But still the dog stared at me and began padding in my direction.

"Garth, come here!" the baron roared with such force that, with a final glance at me, Garth turned and slunk away. The jingle of spurs and clatter of claws passed into the corridor and died away in the distance.

The king sighed heavily, and I heard him leave too. When he had gone, I ran from the room on trembling legs. Instead of searching for Alinor, I crept out of the castle and went home.

Again I wrote much in my book that night.

CHAPTER 8

Early the next day Charles Judde sent me down to the market for a new axhead. As I left the ironsmith's shop I spotted Alinor making her way through the crowds from one stall to another. "There you are," she said when I approached her.

"Where did you go yesterday?" Her voice sounded puzzled and surprised.

"Can I walk you home?" I asked. "I've got to talk to you."

"Sure." She held up a small leather bag that jingled. "But I'm going to your place. I need to pay your stepfather for the baroness' chest."

On the way I told her everything that I had overheard in the Great Hall. Then I asked, "What do you think will happen?"

"I'm not sure. Grandpa doesn't like war. He'll fight if he has to, but you'd be surprised at some of the ways his wars turn out. He's a very creative man."

When we reached my foster parents' home, I was startled to see Charles's four-wheeled cart parked in front, with Max, who's always been good with horses, hitching two ponies to it.

"What's the cart for?" I asked him.

"I don't know. Dad just said to get it ready."

Charles Judde came out of the house. "Dad, where are you going with the cart?" Max asked when he spotted him.

The man grinned. "Make that 'we.' You're coming, and Denis, too." He glanced at Alinor speculatively. "And you can come, too, young lady, if you want to." He chuckled. "We're going for a ride in the country."

"Where to, Dad?" Max persisted.

"The baron's castle."

"Wow!" The boy's eyes shone. "Really? What for?"

"It's tax time. I've got one of the biggest carts in town, so the government picked on me, just like last year. One of the baron's knights knocked on the door a little while ago and ordered me to go pick up the baron's grain tax and take it to the king's castle."

"But—" I started to say, and Alinor's blue eyes hit me like two crossbow bolts.

"What's that, Denis?" Charles asked absently, giving a final tug to the harness buckles.

"Nothing. Uh—how far is it?"

"About five miles. You got something else to do?"

"No, no," I said hastily. "Can you come, Alinor?"

"I guess so. Just let me take this money to Mistress Judde." A few minutes later she climbed into the wagon with the rest of us.

The ride was slow, but still exciting. I'd been on this road before, but never as far as we were going today. To me, the baron's castle had always been a cluster of dim gray towers on a faraway hill.

As we approached, I was awestruck. The castle was larger

than I thought. Gray and massive, it was built on several levels of a high hill. "This is even bigger than the king's," I said.

Charles snorted. "That's right. The king just lets the baron do what he wants with his own property. He'd never get away with building it that big if we had a different ruler. In other countries, if a baron builds his castle too big, the king knocks it down."

"How come?" Max asked.

"Because if the baron's castle is too big, he might rebel."

Alinor's elbow pressed warningly against mine.

"Do you think our baron will revolt, Dad?" Max continued.

His father snorted again. "Who knows?"

He paused suddenly and looked at Alinor thoughtfully for a moment. "Changing the subject for a second, just who are you, anyway?"

Alinor glanced quickly down. "I'm living with the baroness this summer."

"H'mmm," Charles said, returning his attention to the road. "Denis, you were right, that is a big castle." He squinted. "That tower on the left looks new. New stones, I think. And he's widened the moat. I wonder if the king knows about that."

He slapped the reins on the horses' backs to encourage them up the slope. "Sometimes I think the king goes too far in giving people their choices. I think discipline ought to be hard and tough. It's the only way."

Max's eyes widened as they swept over the huge structure. "This beats the king's castle by a mile." He clunked the wagon with his crossbow, which he'd brought with him. "I wish the baron could be king."

Charles twisted around on the seat. Flicking a sidelong glance at Alinor, he roared, "Want me to whip you, boy? That's treason! You shut your mouth."

Max looked surprised. "But Dad, you've always said—"

Charles smacked his son's head so hard that the boy tumbled off his seat. "I said shut your mouth."

Alinor's hand gripped my fingers. When I glanced at her, her face seemed unconcerned, but her fingers were damp and ice-cold. For the rest of the ride Charles kept the conversation on safer subjects.

As I said, the baron's castle stood on a large rock outcropping. The castle walls were tremendously high, notched at the top with crenelations. I knew that behind those toothed openings, running along the inside of the wall, was a sentry walk, a platform on which soldiers could stand and fire longbow or crossbow arrows, and duck behind a crenelation to reload.

At the foot of the hill stretched a wide moat with silvery water. The long drawbridge was down, and beyond it I could see the arched gateway, like a 20-foot tunnel, leading to the interior of the castle.

"Look at the portcullis," Max said as we started over the drawbridge. He pointed at several iron teeth projecting down from a slit in the top of the tunnel. "I'll bet that would kill 10 men if it fell."

"What is it?" I asked.

"It's a big iron gate," Charles explained. "If the enemy manages to make it over the drawbridge, somebody up in the gatehouse cuts a rope and releases the gate. Tough luck for anybody who's underneath when it slams down."

The cart reached the end of the drawbridge and entered

the gateway. As we rode under the portcullis, I looked up apprehensively at its giant iron teeth.

"Dad," Max began as we entered the courtyard, "look at the—"

He stopped short.

Several shouts rang around us. Soldiers seemed to be everywhere. Two leaped to the horses and grabbed their bridles. Others surrounded our wagon.

Charles's face went white. "What's going on?" he asked.

A brilliant sword flashed in the sun, and a soldier placed the point against his throat.

CHAPTER 9

The sun glinted down on the soldiers' shining helmets. No one spoke for a time as they examined us carefully. Finally the tallest one—a sergeant—demanded, "Who are you?"

"Charles Judde, sir."

"What is your business?"

"The king's grain tax, sir. I was told to bring my cart and—"

"Why the children?"

Cautiously Charles wiped sweat off the back of his neck. "To help carry the grain."

"Why didn't you hail when you approached the castle?"

Charles blinked. "I have never hailed before."

"We could have killed you," the sergeant growled. "You must always hail before you enter. If we had been more alert, you might have had the portcullis on the back of your neck."

After giving us one more searching stare, he stepped back. "Proceed. The grain is there." He pointed to a covered shed against the inside wall of the castle.

Slowly the cart creaked forward. Max's face looked slightly green, but I saw him watching the retreating soldiers with admiration. Having relaxed her grip on my hand, Alinor stared around her with great interest.

"Park here, villein," shouted a fat man over by the shed. "Oh. Is that Charles Judde? Good to see you again."

Max's father guided the cart alongside the covered shed. The building had walls about five feet high and a long roof made of loose boards. The fat man and Charles began removing boards, and the sun splashed through onto the grain sacks inside.

"Now, Judde," the fat man said, leaning against the cart, "we wait."

"We do? What for?"

"Because I was told to."

"Just between you and me," Charles whispered, "this place has changed quite a bit since I was here last year."

"Just between you and me, Judde," the fat man replied just as softly, "you're right. The baron approaches!" he yelped, going down on one knee. "Good day, Sire."

The rest of us got hastily down from the wagon and knelt too. The baron approached us on foot across the sunny courtyard. I looked at him with interest. It had been months since I'd seen him, and of course I'd only heard his voice in the Great Hall.

"Good day, villeins!" Though his voice still had that harsh edge, he was smiling. While he was not tall, the massive muscles in his arms and chest beneath his tunic made him seem large and overwhelming. "Rise, please. I understand you are here for the grain tax. Will you be delivering it to His Majesty this evening?"

"If you wish, Sire," Charles answered. "Or I could store it and deliver it tomorrow."

The baron's smile thinned a little. "It is very important that you deliver it today. It must go directly to the castle.

And by the way, some of the grain is not fully cured, so when you deliver it to his grain shed, you must demand that the villein in charge of the shed leave the boards off so the sun can shine through."

The nobleman paused slightly, and Charles's face remained impassive. "And what if it rains, Sire?"

The baron shot a keen glance at him. "The storage shed is under the edge of the wide parapet against the inside north wall. No rain will bother it, yet the sun will reach there."

"I see, Sire."

"Any more questions?" the baron asked, looking sharply at him.

"No, Sire."

"Fine." The handsome smile reappeared. "Now, observe closely. Do you see the brown sacks here?"

Charles craned his neck to look. "Yes."

"That grain is more cured than the grain in these white sacks over here," the nobleman said, pointing.

"I see, Sire."

"So you must put the white sacks on top. And leave the boards off."

"Yes, Sire."

The baron watched as we loaded 12 sacks of grain, five brown and seven white. I noticed that the material used to make the white sacks was finely woven. As I was fingering it thoughtfully, I felt the baron looking at me.

"Boy."

I knelt. "Yes, Sire?"

"Rise. You're a fine young man."

"I thank you, Sire."

"A fine son you have, villein," he said to Charles.

Charles bowed respectfully, then said, "I thank you, Sire, but he is not my son. He is an orphan that my good wife and I adopted."

The baron's eyes flicked over me. "An orphan. And what do you carry in your backpack, boy?"

"A book, Sire. And a pen and some ink."

The man's eyes widened. "Do you know how to write?"

"Yes, Sire."

"How did you learn?"

"I was taught, Sire. By the king's scholar when I was 8 years old."

"Can you write well?"

I lowered my eyes modestly.

"As well as any scribe in the country," Charles said for me.

"Interesting. Villein, what is your name?"

"Charles Judde, if you please, Sire."

"Charles Judde, I am wondering if you are a patriotic man."

Max's father blinked. "I trust I am, Sire."

"The reason I ask is that I am thinking of beginning a new order of squires, to be composed of young villein boys. As you know, no villein can yet become a true knight under normal circumstances. But the training will be the same—with the quintain, the blunted lance, the blunted sword, the shield."

Beside me Max stood motionless, his eyes afire.

"Now, as I look at your young son here—I presume this other boy is your son, right? What is your name, my lad?"

"Max, Sire," my friend breathed.

"As I look at these two boys, I see those in whom I

could find squire material. Is this," and the baron whirled around and snatched up the crossbow from a corner of the wagon, "*yours,* Max?"

The boy opened his mouth, then glanced at his father.

Charles's face turned chalky. "Y-yes, Sire. I know that it is technically illegal to—it is just a toy. It can't harm anyone, so—"

"Can't harm anyone? On the contrary," the baron grinned, "this is a sturdy weapon. Watch." He fumbled on the floor of the wagon for a bolt, held it between his teeth, and proceeded to cock the crossbow by hand. Max gasped.

"Do you see that pigeon?" The baron pointed upward to one of the battlements where a bird perched against the blue sky. We nodded, speechless.

He notched the bolt and raised the crossbow to his shoulder, then stood in silence a moment as though calculating the bow's accuracy before squeezing the iron trigger bar. There was a deadly whizzing sound, and up on the wall feathers burst from the bird like an exploding pillow.

"If you will allow me to train your son Max to use this," the baron said, placing the crossbow in Charles's trembling hands, "I will forget that you have committed the illegal act of making it.

"And you, sir," the baron continued, turning his masterful smile full on me. His voice had more of the harsh ring I'd heard in the Great Hall yesterday. "Do you want to join our little order? With your writing skill, you could be our historian. I will need you to write letters and documents for me."

My heart seemed to stop as he smiled down at me. I looked away, and then up again into his eyes. The world stood still.

CHAPTER 10

Suddenly from behind me came a strange sound. Hunnnhh. Hunnnhh. Hunnnhh.

The baron glanced over my shoulder curiously. I turned to follow his gaze.

Alinor's blue eyes were watering as she pressed her index finger to the bridge of her nose. "Hunnnhh, hunnnhh . . ."

She began to turn away from us. "Ahh-ahhhhh—choo!"

The baron chuckled. "Bless you, young wench. What a forceful sneeze for such a beautiful lady. I apologize for the grain dust. Tell me what I may call you."

"Alinor, sire," she replied in a foggy voice. "I have the honor of staying with your wife for the summer."

"My wife?" he said, then chuckled. "If I visited my town-house more often I would have met you. I haven't been there for several weeks. Been too busy here. Well," he continued, "I must be about my business. I will speak more about my new squire's order at the fair next week." He turned to Charles. "You will remember about the grain? White sacks on top and boards off the shed to let it cure. Goodbye."

As he turned away, we relaxed and began loading grain sacks. Suddenly I saw out of the corner of my eye that the baron had approached us again to stare at the girl, who still stood beside the wagon.

"Alinor?"

"Yes, Sire?"

"That is your name?"

"Yes, Sire."

"You are not a village girl, are you?"

"I'm from Wyndhamshire, Sire."

"Wyndhamshire." For a moment more he looked at her narrowly, then grinned again. "Goodbye."

On the way home Max acted like somebody had given him his own castle for a birthday present. His father tried to bring his dreams down to earth, but the boy kept talking. "I will become a knight, Father. I will."

"You heard the baron. No peasant becomes a knight."

"It's happened before."

Charles glared at his son. "Where?"

"In war. Sometimes peasants are knighted on the battlefield."

"Oh, of course, on the *battlefield*," Charles repeated. "But thank goodness you'll probably never see a battlefield."

"But Dad, you've always said a good war clears the air."

The man brooded awhile, then slapped the reins against the horses' backs a little more sharply than necessary. "Listen, boy, and listen good. War is all very fine to dream about, but when somebody starts shooting crossbows and longbows and catapult stones at you, you'll change your tune."

"I won't," Max insisted. "I'm determined to learn how to be a knight. And if that means going to battle, that's where I want to go."

"Max, we won't discuss it any further," his father said darkly. "A good war may clear the air, but right now I happen to like my air the way it is." He cleared his throat.

"When I saw the baron shoot that pigeon with the crossbow, the same crossbow I made for you, I thought to myself, 'That does it. That thing is no toy.'"

Max knew when to shut up. Although the thrust of his chin showed his stubbornness, he knew that if he had a ghost of a chance of keeping the crossbow, he'd better not stir his father up anymore.

Tactfully changing the subject, I said, "I wonder what's so special about this grain," thumping my fist on one of the white sacks.

"That's what I can't figure out." Charles glanced around doubtfully at the sacks. "You're the scholar around here. Can you read what it says on the bags?"

"I don't see any writing."

"There. Turn over the top one a little."

I did. "That's not writing. At least not writing I'm familiar with. Just a lot of black boxes drawn with a brush."

"That's Chinese," Alinor interrupted.

"How do you know?" Max asked her.

"In Wyndhamshire I'd go down to the silk shops, and some of the scarves would have Chinese writing on them."

"And it looked like this?" I asked.

"Yes. I'm sure it's Chinese."

"What does it say?"

"I can't read it."

"But you're sure it's Chinese?"

"Yes."

Charles grunted. "It must be pretty strange grain. But I guess we do what the baron says."

The rest of the way to the king's castle we rode mostly in silence. Charles hunched moodily forward, whistling a folk dance tune. Max, with a faraway look in his eye, stroked the shaft of the crossbow while Alinor stared thoughtfully at the grain sacks.

When we reached the king's castle, I noticed how small it was compared to the baron's. As we rolled over the drawbridge, I glanced ahead at the archway leading to the courtyard. That's weird," I said aloud.

"What's weird?" Max demanded.

"No portcullis."

Max squinted incredulously. "Of course there's a portcullis. You can't have a castle without a portcullis."

"I can't see one," I said, shading my eyes.

"But there's a slot for one," Max persisted. "It's got to be up in there somewhere."

As the wagon rumbled through the arch we both stared upward into the blackness of the slot.

"See?" I said.

"That's crazy," Max said, lowering his voice. "I wonder if the town knows that the king of the country doesn't have a portcullis in his castle. How does he expect—"

I shushed him as a castle servant approached across the deserted courtyard, now mostly in shadow because of the lateness of the day.

"The baron presents the grain tax to His Majesty," Charles called to him.

"Good," the servant answered. "Drive your wagon over to this shed." I saw that the king's storage shed looked almost exactly like the baron's, and was in the same north position against the inside of the wall.

"We have special instructions about the white sacks," Charles explained. "They are to be piled on top of the pile, and the boards are to be left off the shed. The grain still needs to be cured."

"Thank you. Chinese grain, I see."

"I believe so," Charles said.

"The king will be interested."

CHAPTER ELEVEN

"My advice to you . . ." Max began, grabbing my backpack strap and yanking on it.

"I don't need your advice," I told him cheerfully.

" . . . is to leave that old leather bag at home for once."

"Keep your grubby fingers to yourself." Again I spoke cheerfully, not really meaning any harm.

How could anyone be irritable on the first day of the fair? Max and I were striding along a cobblestone street toward the baron's townhouse where Alinor stayed to see if she'd join us. Charles and Magda would come later, riding in the wagon with some of Charles' finest furniture for his fair booth. Max was fuming because his father had refused to let him take the crossbow.

"If the constables saw you carrying that thing around," Charles had said, "I'd get in trouble. They're illegal."

"Lots of boys have them," Max had wailed.

"Not legally. And not as powerful as yours."

So now as we walked along, my friend was still mad. "My dad's a coward," he growled.

"You're lucky he didn't make firewood out of that bow."

Max snorted. "Well, at least he can't stop me from joining the baron's order."

"He can jolly well stop you if he wants to."

"No, he can't."

"Yes, he can."

Max glared at me. "Not if the baron gets to be king."

"What do you mean, if the baron gets to be king?"

"If the baron gets to be king, crossbows will be legal. A whole lot of things will be different."

I glanced around. "Watch your mouth, Max."

"You watch yours, you loony scribbler."

"Hey, listen, why don't you just turn around and go back home and get out of bed on the right side?"

He said nothing, but just stumped along beside me, breathing heavily. "And," I continued seriously, "you better not spread that baron-king garbage around the fair. That's treason."

"Oh, stick your head in your backpack," he told me. "Since you brought it along, why don't you use it for something useful and smother yourself?"

"Quiet. Here comes Alinor."

"'There's Al-i-nor,'" he mimicked. "'Here comes my sweet Al-i-nor.'"

I ignored him. "Hi, Alli," I called.

Max looked at me with round, mirthful eyes. "Alli?" he whispered. "So we've gotten as far as sweet little nicknames, have we?"

My own eyes dared him to unleash the snicker he was planning. He might be good with a crossbow, but I could beat up on him if I had to, and he knew it.

For some reason she decided to walk right beside me. Max took up a position ahead of us, and I could tell that he was storing up all sorts of things to tease me about later.

"Denis," she asked me, "are you going to have to help Master Judde in his booth?"

"Yes, he is," Max answered from up ahead. "And don't try running off either, Denis."

"I'll have to help some of the time," I said to Alinor. "But I'll get time off. What are you going to be doing? Will you be with the baroness?"

"Probably. She really loves to shop."

"Will the baron be at the fair today?" Max interrupted.

"Yes. He's opening the tournament this afternoon."

Max looked alertly over his shoulder at us. "Did you say this afternoon? Is that when the tournament starts?"

"I think so."

"But the tournament isn't usually until the last day."

Alinor's voice was expressionless. "The baron has organized a tournament for every afternoon of Fair Week."

Max's mouth fell open. "I never heard about that."

"Neither did I," she said drily, "until the baroness told me about it this morning."

"Boy, this is fantastic," Max exclaimed.

"Was this the king's idea?" I asked.

"No," Alinor answered quickly.

Max looked at her curiously. "How do you know?"

"I mean, I don't think the king approves. But he likes to give people their choices, so—"

Max's snort interrupted her. "I'm glad *somebody* has the military good of the nation in mind."

"Cool it, Max," I began. "The—"

"I'm serious. Look up there." He pointed to the gray mass of the royal castle looming mistily above the town. "That place is falling apart. You saw it, Denis. So did you, Alinor. The catapults and crossbows need new twine. The walls need repair. There's not even a working portcullis."

"So what?" I asked.

"What if we were attacked by another country? We'd run to the castle, and there'd be no protection for us."

"The king's servants could pull the drawbridge up," I protested.

"I'll bet it doesn't even work," he insisted. "Have either of you ever seen the drawbridge in a raised position?"

We said nothing for a few moments.

"I wonder how many people will come to the fair," Alinor said, changing the subject.

Max made a disgusted noise with his tongue. "I don't know about you two, but I'm going to take in all the tournaments I can this week. Because who knows? One of these days," he said darkly, "the only thing that might be standing between you and some heathen barbarian is my crossbow."

We were close to the fair now. I could see the colorful pennants rising above the striped tents. A distant horse neighed, and I heard a few notes on a trumpet.

"They're setting up for the tournament!" Max exclaimed, breaking into a run and disappearing up the winding street.

Alinor and I continued walking slowly together. "Denis," she finally said.

"What?"

"Grandpa likes you."

I turned to look at her. "The king? He's probably forgotten I even exist."

"No. He talks about you often."

"Me? How come?"

"He knows you like to write."

I watched her eyes carefully. "What's it to him? So far, my scribbling hasn't got me much respect anywhere else."

"Except at the castle."

"Oh?"

"Sir Robert was amazed at your penmanship."

I paused uncertainly, then said, "Well, thanks for passing on the compliment."

"Grandpa wants you to do him a favor."

"What possible favor could I do His Majesty?"

Alinor paused. Then she looked directly at me and said, "He wants you to have your own booth at the fair."

CHAPTER 12

"M y own booth?" I gaped at her. "What do you mean? Doing what? I have nothing to sell."

"You won't be selling anything," Alinor explained. "You'll get a small daily wage from the king for your trouble, but not from anything you sell. What you will be doing will be given free."

"And what's that?"

"All you have to do is to sit at your booth and teach people how to write."

I stared at her. "Teach people?"

"Sure."

My mouth opened and shut a couple of times. Then I said, "But I'm not a scholar."

"You told me that you showed Mr. Judde's wife how to make letters."

"Yeah, but that's different. I just wrote letters, and she copied them. I can write, but I don't know how to teach it." Shaking my head, I said, "Alli, I'd better not say yes."

"Please." She put her cool fingers on my arm. "It is very important to Grandpa."

"No. Please." Again I shook my head. "I respect His Majesty too much to ruin something that's very important to him."

"You won't ruin it," she insisted.

"How do you know?"

"Denis, he doesn't want you to work miracles or anything like that. He just wants you to sit at your booth and be prepared to show people what you do so well."

In spite of myself, I began to feel a tingle of excitement along my spine. Imagine—me, a humble peasant urchin—having my own booth! During the day I would sit under the canopy behind a counter waiting for customers. And at night I would go behind a canvas curtain to the private quarters at the back, and there I could light a candle and write for as long as I wanted. If I had a small wage I could buy enough candles to light two or even three at once, so I could see better.

But chasing the tingle of excitement was a little rat of fear. Because of my fondness for Alli I didn't want to be disgraced. "Can I think it over?"

"Sure. It's up to you. Grandpa said it's your choice."

As Alinor and I walked through the streets, I was amazed to see how Fair Week had changed the appearance of our sleepy town. It had roused itself, and now the shops and homes were ablaze with colored pennants and tassels. People milled everywhere. Farmers tugged at ropes tied to the nose rings of giant oxen. Children ran by with chickens under their arms. Shopkeepers loaded wagons to take their wares to the booths in the town square.

"Is this like Wyndhamshire?" I asked Alinor as we threaded our way between animals and people.

"Too much like Wyndhamshire," she shuddered.

"What do you mean, too much?"

"I like it more peaceful."

Although I didn't say anything, I liked it more noisy. A lot of times our town bored me to death.

Finally the street brought us into the square where I spotted Charles's cart in front of a big canvas booth. He and Magda were tightening the ropes supporting it.

"It's about time, Denis," Charles roared. "Where's Max?"

"I don't know. We were all walking together, and then he ran ahead."

"Here, help me unload."

Quickly we hoisted the heavy chests and chairs and tables off the cart, and arranged them artistically underneath the canvas roof. "Now, Denis," Charles said to me when we'd finished, "I'll need you to stay here and man the booth this afternoon. Magda and I are going back for a second load, and then we'll be boarding up the house, since we'll be here all week."

I glanced at Alinor.

"Denis can't help you, Mr. Judde," she said.

My foster father eyed her, startled. "Why not?"

"Denis has his own booth."

Charles glanced at me with mild annoyance. "Knock it off, you two. This is no time to tease an old man."

"She's right. I guess it's an order from the king."

"The king?"

"Yes, sir," Alinor explained. "Sir Robert was at the baron's townhouse this morning and told me to tell Denis."

"Wait a minute," Charles said, scratching his head. "Denis, what would you possibly do in a fair booth?"

"It's his writing, sir. The king wants him to sit at his booth and demonstrate how to write, and to teach people if they wish to learn."

"And about time, too," boomed Magda, who had just emerged from the back of the booth. "This should have been done at the fair years ago. The fair is where you catch the people—and catch 'em in a good mood."

Charles was still struggling with this novel idea. "A booth? To teach writing?"

"Denis," Magda announced, "I will be your first pupil. I'll sit there and really show an interest, and that will help other people get over their shyness. I think it's a splendid plan. I'd like to get Max going on this."

"Max!" Charles shouted as though he had just been reminded of something. "Where is that boy? If Denis is going to go off and sit in a booth, who's going to watch my shop?"

"Oh, I'll stay, Charles," his wife said. "You can handle things at home all right."

Sir Robert waited for us across the square where he stood in front of a small new booth with freshly painted canvas and brilliant red and blue pennants fluttering from the front poles. A sturdy wooden chair sat behind a low, flat counter, and three or four chairs had been placed in front.

"Good day, Master Denis," he said, smiling.

"Good day, Sir Robert," I responded politely. Even though he was smiling, I've got too much peasant blood in me to feel perfectly comfortable around nobles. Except Alinor.

"I hope you've chosen to demonstrate your superb writing ability," he said anxiously.

"Well, I guess I could try."

"Thank you," he said, relief in his voice. "His Majesty would appreciate it very much. Here on your counter I've stacked several hundred sheets of the best-quality paper. Use as much of it as you wish. Here is your cake of ink, and several quill pens. There is a large sack of quills and more ink behind the curtain in your private quarters."

"Sir Robert?"

"Yes?"

"Exactly what should I do?"

He smiled broadly. "Just sit at your table and start writing."

"And when someone comes?"

"Ask them if they would like to learn to write the alphabet. Let them try a pen. Offer to write a brief letter to a distant family member for them."

"I—I've never done this kind of thing before."

Sir Robert clapped me on the back. "You'll do fine. His Majesty has taken a liking to you. Oh. He might be by to see you one of these days. And one more thing—" He reached into a little bag at his belt and set a silver coin on the counter. "Today's wages." With a final smile and nod, he left.

In a daze, I sat down in the chair under the canopy and immediately felt a little more important. The canvas smelled new and the wooden chair reminded me of a throne.

I looked out into the busy square. It was nearly noon, and I was getting hungry. Vendors strolled around selling everything from small loaves of bread to pancakes covered with strawberries and cream.

Slowly I unstrapped my backpack, took out my book, and laid the pack safely under the table.

Feeling a little silly because up to now I'd always done my writing in private, I used my knife to sharpen and slit one of the quills. Then grinding some ink powder, I mixed it in a little bowl with water from a water jug (Sir Robert had thought of everything!), opened my book to the next blank page, and began to write.

How long I wrote, I don't know. But suddenly I heard a tremendous *whack,* and the entire counter trembled. A gleaming silver sword point had cut into the table just two inches from my right wrist.

CHAPTER 13

The sun caught the brilliant sword point and sent a hypnotic blue flash into my eyes. It was only after a dazzling second or two that I allowed my eyes to travel up the length of the blade, past the carved metal handle, and finally up the arm and into Max's mischievous gaze. "Hey," he said, withdrawing the sword. "Whose booth is this?"

"Mine." I cleared my throat. "And whose sword is that?"

He grinned. "Mine."

"Can't be."

"Yes, it is."

"Where did you get it?"

"I bought it."

"You don't have money enough for a sword like that."

Max looked around. "Actually, it looks better than it is. There's an armor maker in Milagro the baron knows about, and these are the swords his apprentices practice on when they're learning to make weapons. They're called seconds because they've got flaws." He pointed to where the blade joined the handle. "See there? If I were to really smack you with this it would break." He sighted along the blade. "In fact, it looks like I bent it when I whacked the counter here."

"But where did you get it?"

"Like I said, the baron ordered a bunch of these from Milagro. One of his knights is selling them to guys like me who want to get some experience."

"But they're illegal to someone your age," I protested.

Max looked disgusted. "No, they're not. A real sword is illegal. These flawed ones aren't."

"Yours didn't sound too flawed when you hit my table with it. You could have chopped my hand off."

"Lucky for you I didn't."

I frowned at him. "Listen, Max, what's gotten into you? Ever since your dad made you that crossbow you're really a pain to be around. I wish you'd get that stupid knighthood stuff out of your head."

His lips whitened. As though he were repeating a formula he'd learned, he said, "You have offended my honor. I challenge you to a duel. The choice of weapons is yours."

Groaning, I buried my head in my hands. "Knock it off, Max. Will you just knock all that stuff off? You're talking like a fool."

Drawing in his breath, he intoned, "I summon you to a duel at sunrise tomorrow—"

"Get out of here," I said flatly. "I'm busy."

Finally he dropped his weird manner. "Denis, you idiot. What are you busy at, anyway? Whose booth is this?"

"I told you, it's mine."

"Yours?"

"By order of His Majesty."

He snorted. "You're lying. What possible use could you be to anybody?"

If we'd been at home I would have vaulted over the table and laid him out, but I knew that wouldn't go well in the middle of the square. After all, I was now in the king's service. So I simply said, "I know how to write."

"So what?" he sneered. "Who cares about writing?"

"The king does."

"Enough to set you up in a booth at the fair?"

"That's right."

"I don't believe you."

"Sir Robert was here a half hour ago. He's the one who got this booth ready, the paper and the ink, and everything."

Max stared at me. "Really?"

"Really."

"It's a plot," he declared.

"What are you talking about?"

"It's a plot to weaken the populace. This country is already so unprepared it's pitiful. And now this."

"Unprepared for what?"

"To fight, you moron!" Gripping the sword handle, he swept it around behind him in a dramatic gesture, the sun flaming from its blade. He also came close to beheading an old man hobbling past the booth.

"Watch it," I shouted.

"Shut up," he growled, though I noticed that his hand trembled as he saw the old man's bald head retreating. "Do you know how many active knights the king has?"

"Five."

"Four," he corrected me. "The baron, on the other hand, has 15. The baron of Milagro has 30 or so. Even the baron of Costello has 30. What kind of king won't even prepare his country for battle?"

"Don't ask me," I snapped. "You seem to be the expert."

"What you need to do, Denis," Max said intently, leaning over the counter toward me, "is to join the baron's new order. Forget this writing stupidity—or at least use it for the baron rather than the king."

"Max," I replied firmly, "you keep your nose out of my business, and I'll keep mine out of yours. OK?"

He pointed a trembling finger at me and drew back his sword with his right hand. "Just tell me, smart guy, just tell me what you would do if I were to run you through with this?"

I gazed at him. "You're not going to run me through with that."

"But what would you do if I did?"

"If I knew you would do a fool thing like that, I'd stay out of your way. Or—"

"Or what?"

"Get a sword of my own."

"Exactly." He smiled triumphantly, like a cat who's been given a fresh sardine. "You have just proved my point. You have just bought into the knightly system."

"No, I haven't."

"Yes, you have. The knightly system is merely self-defense. I am preparing myself so that I would know exactly what to do if somebody tried to run me through with a sword. And my advice to you"—and again he raised his sword— "is to go to the armor maker's booth and buy yourself one of these."

"Indeed."

The deep voice that spoke came from right beside us.

When I glanced up, my mouth dropped open. Max whirled around, stared, and dropped to one knee. I was out of my chair in an instant, kneeling too.

"G-good day, Your Majesty," Max quavered.

"Good day, Your Majesty," I echoed.

The king wore a purple tunic with leather leggings. The double belt at his waist had a ring loop for a sword sheath, but he had no sword. He was hatless, and his silver hair gleamed in the sun. Behind him stood Sir Robert and a castle page.

Even as we discovered his presence, others in the square noticed it too. Cries of "His Majesty approaches," "Make way for the king," and "Long live the king" arose from all sides. Peasants removed their hats, and those closest curtsied or knelt.

The king looked around, his eyes crinkling in a kindly smile, and he lifted his hand in a salute. "Rise, please. Welcome to the fair. Please continue your business, and may your week be prosperous." Then he turned back to face us.

"Rise, please," he said again, since we were still kneeling. We stood.

The king looked down at Max's sword. "A big weapon for a small lad," he observed. He squinted at it. "And with a flaw, too. You may wish to warn your father that this sword will do him no good in self-defense."

"This sword is mine, Sire."

The world seemed to grow very still.

"Yours?" the king asked.

"Yes, Sire."

"And where did you get it?"

"I, uh, I bought it, Sire."

"Here? At the fair?"

"Yes, Sire."

The king turned to Sir Robert. "Robert," he said, "this is a Milagran second. Why are we allowing Milagran armorers into our fair?"

Sir Robert's eyebrows raised. "I was not aware of this, Sire."

The king turned back to Max. "Young man, you will answer my questions truthfully. Where did you get this sword?"

CHAPTER 14

"I—I bought it from the armorer's booth, Your Majesty," Max stammered.

The king looked puzzled. "I authorized no armorer's booth."

"The baron authorized it, sire. He ordered seconds from a Milagran armorer, and he's selling them to peasant boys who are interested in knighthood."

Sir Robert frowned. "Your Majesty, should I—"

"No," the king interrupted. "Patience. We must have patience." Then he glanced down into Max's face. "Boy," he said seriously, "I urge that you use this weapon with care."

Max's eyes fell. "Yes, Sire."

And then the king departed as suddenly as he had come, Sir Robert and the page following him. Max wandered off, a little weak about the knees, his sword dangling from a ring at his belt.

But I wasn't alone for long.

"OK, Denis, now's your chance," Magda's voice boomed. She had left her furniture booth and was hurrying over to where I sat. "I told you I was going to be your first pupil, and here I am. Let's see. Where did we leave off last time?"

"What about your booth?" I asked.

"Oh, fiddle on the booth," she snorted. "I can see it from here. If somebody tries to make off with a canopy bed, I hope they break their back. OK, where's the ink?"

She grabbed for a quill pen. "I think I remember how to do an A." She bent over a sheet of paper, thrust her tongue out the side of her mouth, and worked for a few seconds. "There. Is that it? Close?"

"Pretty close."

"Isabel!" she bellowed, waving the quill wildly in the air and catching me neatly in the left eye with a drop of ink. "Come here!"

An anxious-looking woman who'd been examining one of Charles's chairs wandered over and peered at what Magda had written. "What is it?" she asked.

"That's an A," Magda announced proudly. "And I can do it again. Watch. Oh, this crazy pen. *There.*"

"Beautiful," Isabel breathed.

"You try it," Magda encouraged. "Denis, set her up with a pen. Joan! Margaret!"

And in no time at all 10 or 12 women had crowded around my counter, doodling on the paper, making blots, getting ink on their faces, begging me to show them how to write their names, their husbands' names, and their babies' names.

"Well, Denis," said the woman named Joan, "how did you ever learn to write?"

I told them the story of the king's scholar, and some of their faces sobered and hardened.

"I remember him," Margaret said. "He was a sly one, he was."

"I think he was a spy," another added.

"I took just one lesson from him," spoke up someone

called Cecily, "and that was plenty. It wasn't the writing I minded so much. It was what he wanted us to write."

Several gasped in excitement. "What was it?"

"Oh, those crazy rules nobody can figure out. 'Tear down your castle,' and all that sort of nonsense. A busy woman doesn't have time to fool with all that misty-wisty philosophy. So I stopped going to the class right then and there. I told myself, 'I'm not going to get sucked in to any conspiracy.'"

"Balderdash!" Magda replied promptly.

Cecily flushed. "So much for you, Magda. I didn't see you in the class."

"I wish I'd gone."

"But listen," Cecily continued, "the rule I was most suspicious of was the one that says, 'Be fearlessly honest with your king and yourself.' Now, if that isn't the last straw, I don't know what is."

"What's wrong with that one?" Magda asked stoutly.

"Use your head," Cecily snapped. "Don't you know what would happen to me if I was totally honest to the king's face? If I told the king just a tenth of what I thought of him, he'd have me in that dungeon underneath his castle so quick you couldn't say boo."

"That's for sure," another woman scowled.

"I think he's more tolerant than that," Magda said. "And some of those rules aren't as cockamamie as they seem to be. Take the one that says, 'Go to the mountain before you answer; go again before you act.'"

"Who has time for riddles like that?" Joan snorted.

"I finally figured that one out," Magda persisted. "It was one day a few years ago when Charles and I were having a fight. It was New Year's Day, and he wanted mashed turnips with butter and cabbage for lunch. I told him I was planning on bread and soup. He said no, he wanted mashed turnips."

"Isn't that just like a man?" one woman moaned.

"I'd have thrown a fit," another added.

Magda nodded. "And so would I, normally. But this time I said to myself, *Let's use a little common sense here, Magda.* I asked Charles why he wanted mashed turnips. For a while he wouldn't tell me. But finally he came out with it: his mother had always served them for lunch on New Year's Day."

"But that's not saying you have to give in to him," Anne protested.

"Listen for a minute, will you, Anne?" Magda said patiently. "His mother had died just a few weeks before, and I guess this was one way he could remind himself of her. Sort of preserve her memory. So every year since then we've had mashed turnips on New Year's Day."

The other women were silent for a moment. Then one said, "But what does that have to do with going to the mountain? What mountain?"

"Aha." Magda's eyes gleamed. "I still remember when it was that it clicked. I was mashing boiled turnips, and it hit me. What happens when you climb a mountain?"

"You get tired," Margaret said. "And then there's the whole way back down again."

"I mean besides getting tired."

"You can see a lot farther?" Joan suggested.

"Exactly! Here I was living in my own little shell, just thinking about myself, when all this time Charles was feeling bad about his mother. And I didn't know it. I would have never found out how he was feeling unless I'd gotten outside myself—gone up the mountain—and looked over into his life and tried to see what he was thinking. It changed everything."

One or two nodded thoughtfully.

The afternoon began to turn into evening, and one by one the women drifted away to feed their families or to return to their booths. Beginning to feel hungry myself, I thought about closing down the booth and using my silver coin to buy supper from a vendor. Max and some other guys drifted by, yelling at me to come and see the puppet show.

"What puppet show?" It was the first I'd heard of it.

"The baron brought in a troupe of Milagran puppeteers," Max explained. "Come on."

"I haven't eaten yet. Go ahead."

They tramped off to the other side of the square where a long line of people was forming.

"Hello, Denis." Alinor appeared at my counter, holding something wrapped in a cloth. "Did you have a busy afternoon?"

"Yeah. Lots of people came by. Mostly because of Magda."

She grinned. "Good. Grandpa will be pleased. Here," she said, unwrapping the cloth to reveal a covered plate. "I got you some supper."

"Wow! Thanks." When I lifted the lid, the most heavenly aroma I have ever smelled wafted up to my nose. "What is it?"

"I got it from a booth in the next street. It's Asian fried rice and vegetables. You eat it with these." And she gave me two slender sticks.

"With *these*?"

"Yes."

And I did. Don't ask me how. It took me a long time, but with a full-blooded princess standing watching me I sure wasn't going to use my fingers. Finally I finished the rice and put the lid back on the empty plate. "Thank you very much."

"You're welcome. Do you have any plans for tonight?"

"Not really."

"Want to come and see the puppet show with me?"

I hesitated. "Did you know that the baron was the one who hired the troupe? They're from Milagro."

"Yes. That's why I wanted to see it."

Gathering up my book, I slid it into the backpack and slung it over my back. After rolling down the canvas awning, I tied the booth shut. Soon we were seated on a long bench inside a darkened tent at the opposite side of the square.

CHAPTER 15

The puppet tent was dark. At one end, lit by many candles with reflectors, was a small portable stage with its curtains drawn. Probably a hundred people sat in the tent chatting to one another. Then two tinny trumpets blared from somewhere behind the small stage, drums rattled, and a recorder began a haunting whistle.

"Shhh, shhh," hissed a couple of people in the crowd, and the murmuring ceased.

Someone snatched the curtain aside, and the crowd gasped as they saw a beautiful little landscape with lovely green trees and meadows. Far in the distance, on a hill, stood a misty gray castle.

And then onto the stage marched two puppets, dressed in brightly colored clothing. It amazed me how lifelike they looked. I had never seen puppets before. Only by squinting could I see the black threads that held them up.

The story began. It seemed to be set in the East somewhere, and was about a boy named Aladdin who rubbed a magic lamp, and a genie appeared.

"Have you heard this story before?" I asked Alinor.

She nodded. "In Wyndhamshire."

The story wound to a close. It ended with a magical

transformation where Aladdin, dressed in rags, had his garments changed to a rich blue robe at the sound of a loud clap. Watching closely, I saw that there were two Aladdins, and that a swivel trapdoor in the scenery had substituted one puppet for the other.

The curtain closed, and the crowed whistled and applauded. "That was fun," I said to Alinor as I got up to go. "Thanks for inviting me."

"Wait." She motioned for me to sit down again.

And sure enough, another trumpet blast and drum rattle signaled that the show wasn't over. Everyone settled down and the tent became quiet again.

The curtain opened upon the same beautiful meadows and trees. You could still see the misty castle in the distance, but the right half of the stage now resembled the room of a house. On a little bed lay a puppet. From his twitching and writhing we could tell that he was sick.

A tiny, golden-haired girl puppet sat in a chair some distance away. Getting up, she walked jerkily toward the bed, knelt down, and put her arms around the sick puppet.

A sick feeling flooded over me.

Suddenly there was a rattle of drums and a clashing of metal, and onto the stage burst a puppet horse with a puppet knight riding on it. Leaping from the saddle, the knight clanked into the house and seized the little girl and pulled her away from the sick puppet. The puppet on the bed half-rose, reaching out its arms. The little girl screamed in terror, "Father, Father, Father!" and tried to get loose so she could go back to the bed.

But the knight would not let her. Pulling at her, he finally got her outside the house and onto his horse. Wheeling the animal around, he galloped off, and soon the girl's screams died away in the distance.

The audience began to mutter.

Two more puppets came onto the stage, approached the bed, and sadly gathered the ill puppet in their arms. His slack joints and lolling head showed that he had died. They carried him off the stage and then returned.

And then from the left entrance of the stage entered a grand figure wearing a giant crown and long purple robes. His hair was silver. He approached the house where the two puppets stood and spoke to them in a ridiculously high, cruel voice. "Leave this house!" he rasped.

The two puppets begged him to let them stay. They got down on their knees, pleading with him. "No!" he shouted. "Leave! Go away!"

Suddenly the two puppets leaped to their feet and dashed toward the king, kicking him and striking him with their arms. He retreated, still speaking in that harsh voice, until he had disappeared. The curtain closed.

No one applauded this time. The crowd sat in numb silence for a moment or two. And then, as they slowly rose to their feet and shuffled toward the door, I heard a low, sad, angry murmuring begin. To me it was a beautiful sound, a friendly sound, because it expressed exactly what I was feeling.

I hurried away through the crowd.

But then I felt cool fingers on my shoulder. "Denis?"

Shaking them off, I dodged ahead. Once out in the square, I ran to my booth, struggled to untie the flap, and ducked inside.

"Denis?" she said from just outside.

I didn't answer.

"Denis, I saw you go in there. What's wrong?"

Something in my throat wouldn't let me speak, so I said nothing.

"Remember," she said through the canvas, "who hired the puppeteers."

I am sorry to say that at this point I repeated a word that Charles uses when he accidentally strikes himself with his hammer. Again and again I said it, louder and louder.

"I'm sorry, Denis."

I shouted the word once more.

"Come outside," she urged.

We were silent for a while, the canvas wall between us. But the square wasn't silent. The murmuring had turned to angry shouts.

"Then let me come in," she said. "Please. I'm scared."

Fumbling with the flap, I opened it and tied it to the opposite pole. Alinor was kneeling just outside, and she crept quickly in and sat beside me. Now I could see the square clearly, and together we watched as flaring torches placed on stands illuminated little knots of angry villagers talking among themselves. I could see fists occasionally raised.

"Denis, do you think I should tell Grandpa?"

Still I said nothing.

"Talk to me, please, will you?"

Anger filled me now—an anger so tight and terrible that I did not trust myself near her. Still seated on the ground, I turned away from her and began to strike the earth with my fist, first carefully, and then harder and harder.

She waited in silence until my fist hurt so badly I couldn't continue.

" 'Respect those who give you life!' " I shouted. "That's

one of his rules. 'Respect those who give you life!' "

"What do you mean, Denis?"

"That's what the little puppet girl was doing, trying to respect the one who gave her life. And the stupid knight came on his stupid horse and ripped her away from her father!"

"I know."

"You know! Is that all you can say? You *know*?" I snarled at her. "You don't know. You've never knelt at the bedside of your mother and—"

"Denis." Her quiet voice stopped me. "My mother died in Wyndhamshire. Of the plague."

I stared at her. "Oh," I said softly. "I didn't know."

"Well, now you do."

"But did people come and snatch you away from her as she was dying?"

Alinor looked down. "Denis, I don't know why my grandpa does some of the things he does. But one thing I'm sure of—he is a very loving man and cares a lot. He also knows a lot more about things than I do. If he commanded his knights to do that, there was a very good reason."

"Then where does he get off by telling us, 'Respect those who give you life'?"

"I told you, I don't understand everything he does. But I know I'll find out someday when he thinks I'm old enough."

We fell silent again. Outside, the angry discussions had died away, but now a new feeling filled the air. An ugly feeling, a feeling of discontent. A feeling that something was about to burst.

When she finally left, I lit three candles and wrote in my book.

CHAPTER 16

Clang! Clang! Clang!

Magda stood in the square, beating on an iron pot with a wooden spoon.

It was early the next afternoon. I was in my booth leaning back in my big wooden chair, eating a fresh pastry Alinor had brought me from a baker's booth. She sat across from me helping two women and a little dark-haired girl write letters.

"Look," Alinor had said to me earlier that morning.

I was still in a sour mood after the previous night, and I wasn't feeling very friendly. "Look at what?"

She held out her wrist, which was a mottled black and blue.

"What happened to you?" I asked, horrified.

She smiled quizzically at me. "Don't you know?"

"Know what?"

"You really don't know what you were doing to me during that puppet play?"

I stared at her.

"You had hold of my wrist and were gripping it. You squeezed it tighter and tighter."

I hadn't remembered that at all.

Beside me now sat an old man gazing admiringly at a

long letter I had written (at his dictation) to a cousin of his who had moved to Milagro. His cousin probably couldn't read either, but would no doubt find a scholar to decipher it.

"It's time for the game!" Magda called, clanging her iron pot again. "Bring your gifts! It's time for the game!"

Immediately people scurried across the square. My female customers left me. Some women dived back into their booths; others fumbled in great bags they carried with them. The little dark-haired girl and other children began to gather and sit in a large circle at the center of the square.

"What game are they going to play?" Alinor asked me.

"The gift game."

"Are we—all right, Denis?"

"What?"

"Are we still friends?"

"Yeah," I answered curtly. "Forget last night. Sorry I was an idiot."

"I'm not blaming you for your feelings."

"I said, let's forget it."

She opened her mouth to say something, but Magda's powerful voice stopped her. "OK, everybody. Get in a circle. Make it a big one. You kids there—move back, move back. Now, does everybody have their gifts in the middle? Any more gifts?"

She glanced over at the booth where I sat. "Denis! Alinor! Come on and play!"

"I'm going to sit it out," I called.

"Come on, Denis. Be a good sport."

"No!" I replied sharply. "Alli, go ahead."

"But I don't have a gift. Wait." She fumbled at her dress and removed a little wooden pin—a carved flower—ran to the gift pile, placed it there, and sat down in the circle.

"All right," Magda boomed. "You know the rules. I give you each a wood chip from this pot. It has a number on it. Whoever has number 1 will choose a gift and take it back and place it in front of him on the ground. Number 2 chooses another gift from the pile. He either takes it back to his place, or exchanges it with number 1 for his gift."

Magda handed around the iron pot, and each person took a wood chip. Some who didn't know their numbers asked others for help, and soon everyone knew where they stood in the order.

"Number 1!" Magda cried, and the game began.

Usually I enjoyed watching it, but my rotten mood just wouldn't leave me. The puppet show last night, plus the surly anger of the crowd after the performance, had started feelings churning about inside me that I thought I'd left behind long ago.

So it was through a fog of anger that I watched the game today. People had brought all kinds of things. A little boy had brought a baby chick that he prevented from running away by a thread tied to its leg. Others brought old crockery, or wooden boxes, or embroidered handkerchiefs.

Startled to see an old book lying on the pile, I nearly leaped over the counter and joined the game. But when I squinted at it, I could see that it was merely a cleverly carved piece of wood resembling a book.

"Number 7!" Magda announced, and after a whispered question to her mother, the little dark-haired girl shyly arose and began to circle the gift pile. Suddenly she gasped and dived into the pile, emerging with a black object I had a hard time recognizing at first.

Then I saw that it was a stuffed cloth cat. Crudely made and dyed black, the eyes, nose, and mouth were stitched with white thread. Its expression was crooked and a little wild, but the dark-haired girl clutched it to her heart as if it were a real kitty.

She took it back to her seat, cooing over it, and carefully placed it behind her back. Indignant cries rose from some little boys on the other side of the circle.

"No, no, Jana," the girl's mother said. "You've got to put it in front of you so someone else can have a chance at it."

The child's eyes filled with tears, but she slowly placed the cat in front of her.

"Number 8."

The gift trading continued with lots of laughter. Alinor's carved flower was received with delight by an old woman who placed it against her dress admiringly before laying it in front of her.

"Number 17."

A small boy arose, picked something at random from the pile, and walked straight over to Jana. Dropping his gift at her feet, he reached down for the cat.

"No!" the little girl screamed, bursting into tears. Her mother comforted her while the small boy bore the cat triumphantly back to his place.

"Number 18! Who has 18?"

The small boy didn't get to keep the cat for long. Another boy beside him promptly took it from him, and then a third boy. Eyes brimming with tears, Jana followed the progress of the cat as it changed hands.

"Number 27."

Alinor arose, chose something from the pile, and then

walked straight to the boy with the cat. "Thank you," she said, exchanging with him.

Jana looked even more crestfallen than ever. If adults as well as children were trading for the cat, she'd even have less of a chance at it. But I noticed that her mother smiled and nudged her neighbor. The neighbor smiled, and soon winks were traveling around the circle.

"Number 30."

A small boy squeaked in delight. Leaping to his feet, he grabbed something from the pile and claimed the cat from Alinor.

"Thirty-one!"

An old grandmother used her cane to get to her feet, hobbled over, and claimed the cat from the boy.

Now the game became more intense. Without having said a single word, most of the adults had just one object in mind: capture the cat for Jana. But would the numbers run out before the right people had the cat?

"Thirty-seven."

A small boy got the cat.

"Thirty-eight!"

A young man, who apparently wasn't in on the conspiracy, chose a gift from the pile and kept it.

"Thirty-nine," Magda called. She paused. "Thirty-nine. Who's got 39?"

When no one responded, she suddenly looked into her palm. "Wait a minute. I'm 39!"

Amid the roar of laughter that followed, she claimed the cat and gripped it, smiling.

A teenage girl said, "Forty. Aren't you going to call 40?"

Magda blinked. "Was there a 40? OK, 40."

The girl took the cat from Magda's fingers and tossed it to Jana. The child screamed with delight and clutched it to her. And the circle of players clapped and shouted.

I settled back in my chair with relief. And somehow, as the chattering women and children separated, the world became right again.

Just then I heard trumpets in the distance as the tournament began. "Alli," I yelled to her, "want to go see the jousting?"

She rolled her eyes. "No. Is that where you're going?"

"Yeah." Hastily I laced my backpack and strapped it on. "See you later."

CHAPTER 17

"Denis, stop!" Alinor ran beside me.

Pausing, I looked at her wide and tragic eyes. "What's wrong?"

"You're really going to the baron's tournament?"

"Sure. Why not?"

She paused, watching me, then her eyes fell. "That's where my father was killed. In a tournament at Wyndhamshire."

"Oh." I looked at the ground. "I'm sorry."

"Won't you stay here?"

"Alli, I'll be OK." I started on my way again.

"Be safe, that's all I ask," she called after me.

What a girl, I thought as I ran through the streets toward the colored pennants atop the arena. It was too bad about her father, of course. But the way she treated me you'd think she was my mother or something. Or my wife! *Alinor Anwyck.* Now, that was an interesting thought. *Denis and Alinor Anwyck.*

I grinned to myself. *Don't get above yourself, peasant orphan scum. She's blue blood and you're not. You're lucky if yours is even red. Probably you'll end up with some smart little street wench for a wife. If that.*

But Alinor likes me, I thought. *That's something. At least it counts for a little.*

"Watch where you're going, bucky," snarled a rum-soaked voice. Lost in my self-argument, I'd rammed a farmer's huge stomach with my head. Skipping aside before he could clout me, I dived low into the huge mob ringing the arena where I wriggled and squirmed among legs, both bare and cloth-covered. So successful was my burrowing that I popped out on the far side into the tourney area itself.

And there, eight feet away, sat the baron on horseback. He was magnificently armored and was trying to quiet his very jittery steed. As I rose to my feet, the horse's hooves descended to the earth, and the baron looked at me. And then at my backpack.

"My historian!" he roared, causing all eyes to turn in my direction. People backed away in respect. "Come, my boy!" he shouted above the clamor and pointed. "Sit over there, on the end of that bench. Watch carefully so you can write the history of this tourney. Hurry!"

Shyly, my head down, I scurried along the edge of the arena to a long bench. Several huge, half-armored men occupied it, but they left just space enough to squeeze in on the end.

"Hey, little goat," the man next to me protested. His face was grizzled and badly scarred, and he did not appear to have a right ear. "Get off the bench."

"The baron told me to sit here."

"Call me Sir Alex, little goat," he growled. "I'm Sir Alexander Kyriell." He paused as if the name should mean something to me. I dimly remembered Max mentioning him once.

"You're one of the baron's knights, Sir Alex?"

"Yeah." He looked me over again. "What you got on the baron?"

"What do you mean, Sir Alex?"

"How come he sent you over here?"

"I know how to write, and he wants me to write about the tourney."

"You?" Disbelief filled the crags and creases of Sir Alexander's face. "Who taught you?"

"The king's scholar, sir."

His face blackened, and he moved away from me.

The silver-snarly sound of trumpets shocked us all into silence. When I glanced around the arena, I saw it contained nearly a thousand people. At one end of the circular field stood a high covered grandstand where the baroness and other court ladies sat. There was an empty seat near her, and I wondered if Alinor was expected to be there too.

A herald began to call out the combatants. "For the Blues, Sir James Calveley. For the Reds, Sir Gobin Conlin. To your marks!"

I'd never been so close to the action before. Last year I'd had to content myself with watching from a tall tree across the road. From a distance it had seemed so romantic. Now, up close, I saw the sweating horses and heard the heavy jingle of chain mail, and I found myself looking at the blunted lance points and wondering if they were blunt enough.

"Hey, goatlet!" Sir Alexander snapped his fingers at me, chuckling. "Write this down: Gobin is a dead duck."

Sir Gobin, whose horse was draped in a gaudy red blanket, certainly did seem to be less experienced than the other knight. As his horse trotted to the end of the field and wheeled, he actually lost the grip on his lance, and only a desperate snatch prevented it from falling. A few in the crowd hooted.

"Calveley will nail him," said another knight further down the bench.

"Yeah," Sir Alexander replied, "and since I'm on next, I'll have to take on Calveley. Jack!" A smooth-shaven young squire, hearing his name, leaped to his feet and raced toward us, carrying a helmet, a shield, and a bright-red cloak. Sir Alexander stood up and buckled on the helmet, muttering, "Rusty old rain bucket." He wrapped the cloak around his shoulders, clasping it at his throat.

"Jack," he said in a low voice, "get me the sharper lance."

The squire's face was impassive. "Sorry, sir. Blunted lances only."

"Jack, I swear I won't squeal."

"Sorry, sir. The umpire insists."

"Do you dare to—"

"Get out of the way, Alex!" several knights shouted. "We can't see!" Hooves thundered on the field, and Sir Gobin and Sir James clashed together. True to Sir Alexander's prophecy, Sir Gobin got the worst of it. He caught Sir James's lance on his shield, but failed to deflect, and found himself lifted off his saddle and thrown to the ground.

"Here I come, Sir Jimmy," Sir Alexander muttered from inside his helmet.

He mounted the stallion that a stableman held ready, and reluctantly accepted a blunted lance from Jack's hand.

"For the Blues, Sir James Calveley," the herald shouted. "For the Reds, Sir Alexander Kyriell."

The crowd's applause was loud. Apparently both knights were popular. "This'll be a good one," one of the knights on the bench commented to the others. "Somebody's going to get hurt."

Sir James and Sir Alexander rode to opposite ends of the field. At a short trumpet blast they galloped across the turf toward each other. Sir Alexander rode high in the saddle, lance steady despite the leaping steed beneath him. Sir James was equally cool, and at the last moment raised his lance and caught Sir Alexander hard on the helmet. It flew upward and off, and to my horror, I saw a bloody mess where his right eye should have been.

Seven knights on my bench leaped to their feet. "Sharp lance! Sharp lance! Umpire! Check the lance!" They scrambled for their swords and ran onto the field. The Blue knights at the opposite side of the arena leaped into action.

Then into the midst of the fray thundered the baron's horse. "Stop! Stop, you imbeciles! Stop! In the name of the king I command you to cease!"

It was perhaps the four-foot sword that he wielded so expertly, rather than the name of the king, that caused the knights to fall back. The umpires came forward and examined Sir James's lance. Instantly a dispute arose about its bluntness, and while the umpires decided that, several men and boys carried Sir Alexander toward my bench and dropped him roughly on the grass three feet from my foot. His face no longer looked human. It was covered with blood, and his eye—or what had been his eye . . .

Suddenly my head felt light and I began to sweat. Tilting sideways on the bench, away from Sir Alexander, I immediately lost my dinner.

CHAPTER 13

It took a few moments for me to empty myself and get back enough strength to scratch a bit of dirt over the result. When I got up and turned around, I instantly shut my eyes again because the village doctor was doing something to Sir Alexander's eye socket. At the same time I plugged my ears to shut out the knight's agonized groans.

Someone shook me from behind, and, hearing my name, I opened my eyes.

"Denis!" It was Max. "What's wrong with you?"

I opened my mouth to speak, but immediately closed it again. A bit of lunch that had missed the first trip was rising to make its appearance. "Hey, man, calm down," Max said. "This is war."

After gulping a couple of times, I managed, "Did you see his eye?"

"Whose? Sir Alex's? Did he lose an eye?"

"I think so."

"Well, that's the way it goes," he shrugged. "You've got to strap your helmet tight if you want it to stay on."

It's lucky for Max that I was feeling pretty weak right then, or I would have decked him. Even at that I made a grab for him, but the trumpets sounded again.

"For the Blues, Sir James Calveley," the herald intoned. "For the Reds—"

"I'm getting out of here," I said.

"No, hold it," Max urged. "Stick around. You don't want to miss the melee, do you?" And interestingly, I found as I seated myself on the bench that I didn't want to miss the melee. Sir Alexander had been carried farther from the field, cursing and groaning. The melee had been the most exciting part when I'd seen it from the treetop a year ago.

The rest of the one-on-one combats were pretty routine. Nobody else really got injured, even when a horse went down. A horrid snap and an almost human scream from the animal showed that it had broken its leg, and I turned my head away while they put a merciful dagger to the artery in its throat.

And finally came the melee when all the Red knights and all the Blues charged each other like two armies, and fought it out. It followed no order or system. Everybody used lances for the initial clash, but rapidly abandoned them for swords for the close-up combat. The knights were supposed to fight with blunted "seconds," but I noticed several reddened blades swinging in the air.

And then the trumpet sounded for the conclusion, and the crowd applauded and began to drift away. But before they could get too far away, the baron's ringing voice called them back. Again astride his horse, his armor gleaming in the late-afternoon sunlight, he held high his giant sword.

"Attention, all peasants and commoners!" he shouted. "Please, your attention for one minute more. I have something very important to say to you."

He waited while the crowd paused expectantly.

"You have seen today's tournament," he said when the people had quieted down. "You have seen that it has featured many of the bravest knights from here and abroad. You have seen how well they have conducted themselves on the field of honor. I am told that even though Sir Alexander lost an eye in today's combat, he bravely told his squire that he'll fight again at week's end!"

A nearby knight snorted softly. "That's not what *I* heard Alex say," he remarked to another knight. A tremendous cheer drowned his words.

"You have seen," the baron continued, "how bravely the Reds and the Blues entered the lists, and how valiantly they have fought. You see how quickly they would spring to battle for our king if that were necessary.

"But my people, they are not enough. We need more like them! Peasants and commoners, I beg of you your sons. I hereby announce that by my authority as baron, I am creating a new order of squires. If you lend me your sons, by contests and trials I will select the finest and fittest of them to become squires, from which, if knightly blood does indeed run in their veins, they will be knighted by the flat of the sword. The training will be hard, and only a small number will succeed. But I invite all boys between the ages of 12 and 15 to my castle next Monday morning. My knights will give you more information as the day nears. Good day to you!"

A strange sound arose from the crowd. Part of it consisted of a general cheer, but another part was higher pitched—the voices of young boys beseeching their fathers to allow them to go to the trials. Max, of course, was in seventh heaven.

"Denis! Denis! Are you coming along?"

"What, to the trials? I'm better with a pen."

"But the baron wants you to be the historian."

"Well," I said, "I'll see. Maybe so. It depends on how I feel Monday."

He eyed me narrowly. "Don't let your girlfriend talk you out of it."

"Who's my girlfriend?" I glared at him.

"If you don't know by now, you're more of a dolt than I thought you were."

I walked away and returned to my booth, where I found Alinor waiting for me. "You look pale," she said.

"That's probably because I am pale."

"Denis."

"You're different."

"You're not the first person who's told me that," I snapped. "I just left someone else who thinks the same thing."

"You know what I mean."

"*What* do you mean?"

Her upper lip began to quiver, and with a shock I realized that the princess was actually going to cry. I didn't quite know what to do about it.

"Alli," I said patiently. "What do you mean, I'm different?"

"You're—" and she stopped.

"You mean since that puppet show?"

"Yes, but even more than that. Right now. You're—tougher, somehow."

"What are you talking about?"

She faced me, her deep-blue eyes disturbed. "Denis, are you going to go to the baron's trials on Monday?"

I looked away. "Oh, probably."

"Why? You were so against him at one point."

"Alli, look. I love His Majesty the king, and I hope I'm a faithful peasant in his service, but there's a lot of truth in what the baron says."

Now her lips had whitened. "Denis, remember the puppet show."

"What about it?"

"The puppets overthrew their king."

A chill went down my back. "That's right," I murmured. "I'd forgotten that. And that's what the baron hinted might happen when I heard him in the Great Hall."

"Please, Denis. Stay away from the baron's castle."

As I turned away uneasily, I said over my shoulder, "I've decided to go, Alli."

"Then take this."

She held out a small oval mirror about the size of my palm, with thick golden edging. Taking it, I looked at my reflection. It reflected my scowl so well that I changed my expression.

The girl giggled. "The magic mirror: it changes frowns to smiles. Seriously, Denis, I want you to keep this in your backpack. It won't break, because it's protected by the gold. I have one too." She showed me its twin.

"Why do I need this?" I peered into it again. "Is my hair messed up?"

Again she giggled. "Yes, but that's OK. This mirror is for signaling."

"Signaling?"

"Yes. If you do go to the baron's castle Monday, and if something happens to you, signal me by flashing the village with sunlight. If you need me to send help to the castle, signal quickly. But if you'll be able to escape, signal slowly. I'll try to flash you in return. If you signaled slowly, I'll go down to where the twig is, and meet you there."

I gave her a blank look. "What twig?"

"The one you showed me the day we met."

"Oh. That one."

"You'll remember to signal if something *goes* wrong?"

"Alli, nothing will go wrong."

"But just in case?"

I gritted my teeth. "But even if something *does* go wrong, what can you do?"

"Oh, lots of things. I could signal the castle for soldiers or something. Remember: blinking fast means real danger, and slow is simply an alert that we should meet at the twig."

"We're borrowing trouble, Alli."

"Denis, just promise me. I'll be watching all day."

With a grimace I nodded. "Oh, OK. I guess so."

CHAPTER 19

"Fall in!" barked a burly squire.

It was sunrise Monday morning, and Max and I and probably 40 other boys stood in the courtyard of the baron's castle. We'd arrived while it was still dark, and someone had put us under the charge of a group of squires, themselves knights-in-training.

"I said fall in!" the squire snapped as he eyed us sourly. "All right, so you don't know what 'fall in' means. Well, here's what it means. Watch me."

"Fun, fun, fun," I muttered to Max.

"What's that?" The squire's black eyes clashed with mine. "Your name, boy."

"D-Denis Anwyck, Sire."

"I'm not a Sire, I'm 'sir.' When you speak to me, you must always call me sir. The baron and the king are 'Sire'; a squire is 'sir.' Is that clear?"

"Yes, sir."

"Anwyck, there'll be no chatter in formation. Is that clear?"

"Yes, sir."

"When I want chatter from you, I'll ask for it."

"Yes, sir."

"As it happens, I *don't* want chatter from you. Understood?"

"Yes, sir. I mean no, sir. I mean yes, sir."

And so the happy morning wore on. They drilled us on marching, military etiquette, posture, chivalry, everything under the sun besides what we really wanted—weapons training. But finally, just before noon, came the balance-cudgel trials.

In balance-cudgel you place two wooden boxes on the ground about eight feet apart. Then you lay a long wooden board between them. You and your opponent are each given a cudgel—a stout wooden stick about six feet long. You climb up on the board and approach your opponent with cudgel in hand, and you try to knock each other off. Whoever hits the ground first loses.

The squire wouldn't let me take part in the cudgel drills because it's hard on the knuckles if you're not an expert. The baron didn't want my hand ruined for writing. So I wandered around the courtyard watching the balance-cudgelling and enjoying the sunshine.

Several balance-cudgel matches went on at the same time, and I noticed that the baron's grain shed was now open to the sky—the squires had confiscated all the boards.

As I peered into the grain shed, I noticed that the baron still had several white sacks with Chinese writing on them. I had reached over and was prodding one of them when I heard my name called—in the baron's harsh accents.

"Anwyck!"

Instantly I straightened up. "Yes, Sire."

He stood behind me, staring straight at me with no hint of a smile. "Why aren't you at cudgels?"

"My hands, Sire."

"Oh," he said, annoyed at himself. "I forgot. Yes, we do

want to protect your fingers. What are you doing here?"

The question came at me like a crossbow bolt. "Nothing, Sire. Just looking around."

"I'd suggest that in the future you stay with the others. You must get into the habit of staying with the troops. Otherwise you'll be worthless as a historian."

"Yes, Sire."

"But for now, follow me."

I followed a couple of paces behind him as he led me into the castle keep. We ascended a circular staircase, past the floor where his great hall seemed to be, and up into the baronial chambers at the top.

To my surprise I noticed a large number of knights in the chamber and swiftly counted them. All 15. They stood in a circle as if waiting for something.

"Anwyck," said the baron, "you will sit at that table and prepare your writing materials." He pointed to a small writing desk. Opening my backpack, I took out my pen and ink bottle, plus a sheet of the paper I had used at the booth.

"Now," the baron began, "I will tell you what to write. It is important to leave enough space at the bottom for these knights to make their mark. This is a legal document, so write clearly and well."

Then he began to dictate, standing right by my table and watching me carefully. I was pretty sure he couldn't read, but he was smart enough to watch me to make sure that I was really recording what he'd said. He'd say a word, and then watch my hand. It took a long time.

I couldn't understand all the legal language, but I got the main point loud and clear: it was an oath, and if the knights signed it, it meant that they were renouncing all other loyalties, even to the king, and pledging all their allegiance to the baron and the baron only.

Finally I finished the last word and stepped aside. Then one by one the knights came forward and made their marks on the page. None knew how to write, but some had learned to sign their name in a crude way. Others scrawled a complicated design that supposedly could not be counterfeited well. Then the baron clamped a small metal seal to the paper.

"Thank you, Anwyck," the baron said heartily. "You're a very useful young man to have around. I like you." He clapped me on the back. "And now, be off. We've got important things to talk about."

"Yes, Sire." Hurriedly I replaced my pen and ink bottle in the backpack, buckled it on, and left the room.

Just after I'd passed through the doorway, I felt a hard object digging into my back. It was something inside my backpack, and it was so uncomfortable that, in the hallway just a couple of feet beyond the door, I stopped, knelt down, and took off the pack. Just at that moment I happened to glance back into the room and, around the edge of the door, I saw the baron's hands open a large silver box and place the written oath inside. And then I heard him say something that chilled me to my core.

"Cedric," the baron called.

"Yes, Sire," one of the knights replied.

"I want you to be responsible for keeping that little brat here at the castle. Don't let him get away. How you keep him here is up to you. But he must not leave."

"What about his parents?"

"He has no parents—he's an orphan. Nobody will care

if he never comes back. And we don't dare let him out of here. He's a smart little rascal, and if he understood the meaning of what I had him write, he could rat on us to the king. And there would go the revolution."

Several other knights growled in agreement.

"So, Cedric, I'm leaving it up to you. I don't know whether we'll need him to write for us again. I doubt it. But whatever happens, he must not leave here. If you need keys to one of the cells down below, see the steward."

"Yes, Sire."

"And now—all of you—get back to the courtyard and continue the trials."

As feet shuffled within the room, I never felt more scared in my life. Clutching the half-open backpack carefully so that nothing rattled, I dashed along the corridor to the tower staircase, and when I knew I was out of earshot, I began pelting down the steps.

But suddenly I stopped.

The mirror. Alinor. Should I signal her?

Turning, I dashed back up the stairs until I finally burst out into the watchman turret at the top of the keep. Luckily it was empty. Down below I heard the clatter of descending knightly spurs.

Kneeling on the flat stones of the tower floor, I fumbled in my backpack. "Aha," I muttered. The little gold mirror had been the hard object I'd felt. The weight of the book had pressed it against my spine. And if I hadn't stopped just outside the doorway to the baron's chambers, I would never have suspected the plot against me—and would never have learned that the baron was planning to lead his knights in a revolt.

So now I needed to signal Alinor. Clutching it, I rose to

my feet and crossed to the little patch of sunlight streaming in through one of the windows. In the distance I could see the village, 10 miles away. How would I know if I had the flash aimed correctly?

I thought quickly, then leaned out the tower window, put my face in the sunlight, and held the mirror right under my eye with my right hand. Stretching my left arm out toward the town, I pointed at it with my index finger and adjusted the mirror until the bright spot bathed my knuckles in brilliance. Carefully I tipped the circle of light up and down, from my knuckles to the town and back again.

"Anwyck!" A man's sharp voice in the courtyard shouted my name.

The mirror slipped from my fingers and bobbled in midair.

CHAPTER 20

Desperately I reached for the mirror and just managed to nip it between my right thumb and little finger. For an instant it dangled heavily and almost slipped out of my grip. Slowly I drew it upward and clutched it in my trembling left hand. Then I pulled myself back in through the window and crouched down in the corner of the turret.

"Anwyck!" the voice below shouted. "Does anybody know where Anwyck went?"

Suddenly I trembled with relief. Whoever it was down in the courtyard—probably Sir Cedric—evidently hadn't seen me in the tower, but had just been calling for me in a general way.

Now I had less time than ever, and wondered whether I should keep signaling to Alinor. I'd managed to get only one flash off, and if she'd caught it, she'd have no way of knowing whether I was in real danger or not. Agonizingly I tried to decide whether I should risk showing myself again in order to send more flashes.

Carefully I got up on my knees and peeked over the window ledge toward the distant village. I was raising the mirror for another quick try when I saw it—a steady, slow silver winking from a grove of trees near the town. She'd received my message, but thought it was slow rather than fast. That meant no reinforcements from the king's castle.

Suddenly I had a daring idea, one that caused me to quickly replace the mirror in the backpack. But I didn't lace it shut. Silently I hurried down the tower steps, knowing that I needed to move fast before my bravery evaporated.

If I can just get hold of that oath. . . .

In a second or two I reached the floor where the baron's chambers were and casually strolled down the hall. Could the chamber be empty? Pausing outside, I listened above the beating of my heart. Still no sound.

Taking my courage in both fists, I peered around into the chamber. Empty. In a flash I had reached the silver box, struggled with the clasp, opened it, and crammed the oath into my backpack. Then I dashed for the turret again.

When I reached it, the shouting down below had increased. Several knights, and even some of the boys, were yelling my name. Evidently they'd suspected from my absence and my failure to answer their calls that I was up to something. It sounded as though they had suspended the training to hunt for me.

Down the hollow circular staircase I heard a familiar voice. "Maybe he's up here, sir."

Max's voice. "Should I check?"

"Yeah," said a man's voice I couldn't identify. "Check it out, Judde. If you find him, tell him Sir Cedric wants to see him. Tell him to hustle."

I waited until Max was partway up the stairs. Before he'd reached the first floor, I hissed his name and he stopped, wondering where the sound had come from.

"Up here," I said as loudly as I dared. "At the top." Then

I ducked out of sight. His footsteps came closer. As he rounded the final curve of the staircase he looked at me with a puzzled expression.

"Where've you been, man?" he asked. "Didn't you hear everybody yelling for you? Here. Let me tell Sir Boniface that—"

"Stop!" The fright in my voice caused his jaw to drop.

"What's wrong?"

"Max. Listen carefully. I've got to get out of here, and you've got to help me."

His eyebrows came together in a frown. "You look white as a sheet. What's wrong?"

"You don't want to know. It's safer if you don't. Just get me out of here."

His manner changed, and he became very soothing. "Denis, how much time did you spend out there in the sun?"

My fists clenched. "I'm not sick, Max. I don't have sunstroke. I'm just deadly serious when I tell you that I've got to get out of the castle. They're after me."

Carefully watching me, he began to move backward toward the staircase. "Hey, man," he said softly. "Just stay where you are. I'll get help. Do you feel like you have a fever?"

"Max!" My voice quavered, and I strove to tighten it up. He dare not think I was crazy from the sun. "Max, listen. I don't want to have to tell you this, but I will. All of the baron's knights have signed an oath to give allegiance to nobody else but him. And they're planning to overthrow the king."

"Quit babbling, Denis. You ought to be in bed. Just wait here while I—"

"Stop, Max," I gasped. Slipping off my backpack, I fumbled with the lacing. "Wait. I'll show you." A few seconds later I drew out the oath.

"What's that?" he asked, his eyes opening wide.

"Something the baron dictated to me with all his knights present. Let me read it to you." I turned the document so we both could see it—though, of course, he couldn't read—and I went through it word by word. I could see his mind working fast. With this document before him, especially with the metal seal attached, he couldn't very well say that I'd gone crazy.

"Wow" was all he said when I finished.

"Now do you see why I need to get away?"

"No, I don't."

"Use your brain. They've got to keep me here because I'm the only other one besides the knights who knows what the baron is plotting."

"Oh."

"Oh is right. We've got to think of some way I can escape and get to the king." I thought hard. "I've got it. You go downstairs and say you've checked this turret and that I'm not here. By the time you get down there, you'll be telling the truth."

"Where are you going?"

"I'm not sure. But just keep them off my back for a bit."

Still looking at me, he turned and clattered down the stairs. While his footsteps grew fainter, I scanned the roof of the keep. Maybe I could—"

"Judde, is that you?" came a harsh voice from far below in the stairwell. The baron.

"Yes, Sire," Max answered faintly.

"Is Anwyck up there?"

Six heartbeats of silence.

"Judde?"

"Yes, Sire." Max's voice was calm. "He's up there. At the very top. In the turret."

CHAPTER 21

When I heard Max betray me, I suddenly became a cold-blooded animal. A fox. I felt no rage at him then, no tears. I didn't think about that at all. My only desire was to get away. Quickly.

I jumped onto the turret windowsill for a second, then down onto the roof tiles. The roof of the keep was round and pointed, and impossibly steep. *Don't look down, don't look down.* Panic found me footholds, and I scrambled around the roof to the side opposite the turret. If the baron's castle was like the king's, there should be—yes! There it was.

A narrow wooden bridge, like the one Alinor had raced across the first time I visited the king's castle, ran from the baron's chamber high above the courtyard to the crenelated outer wall. Alinor had told me that a bridge like that allowed the ruler of the castle to go quickly from his chambers to the wall to keep an eye on any battle that might be taking place. If attackers managed to climb the wall, the castle's defenders could knock down or burn the bridge, and the keep itself would still be secure.

I scurried to the edge of the roof. It would be about an eight-foot drop to where the bridge connected to the keep. The problem was that the roof overhang made it impossible to see where I'd be landing—whether there was a balcony or not—and if I missed a rooftop, my next stop would be the stone courtyard 60 feet below.

"Anwyck!" roared the distant voice of the baron. He'd evidently reached the turret, and his tone was breathless and panicky. "Anwyck! I need to talk to you. Where are you?" I wasted no more time. Rolling over onto my stomach, I inched my way to the edge of the roof. Desperately gripping the tiles, I allowed first my feet, then my knees, to dangle in midair. What was below me? A glance over my shoulder told me that I would probably drop directly on the bridge. But was there a wider area below, to allow for error?

"Judde!" the baron yelled. "Unchain Garth, quickly! I've got a document Anwyck wrote for me—that'll give Garth the scent!"

I shoved off, and soon I hung by my fingertips. Now I could see below me. A stone platform. I dropped, pitching forward with one great sob against the outer wall of the baron's chamber. Jumping to my feet, I checked my balance, eyed the strength of the bridge, and dashed across it. It creaked beneath me, but I made it to the other side.

And there I found what I was looking for: the release mechanism for the bridge. Quickly I lifted a metal rod, and with a great creaking my end of the bridge dropped away, and the whole thing crashed down into the courtyard.

By the time the echoes had died away, I had dived into a watchman turret 30 feet along the wall and heard shouting below. Then I ran along the wall, in full view, to the next turret, which took me out of sight of the ruins of the bridge. I darted to the next turret and, after listening carefully down its stairwell, descended.

When I reached the courtyard level, I saw that I was

right next to the open-topped grain shed. For a second I debated diving into the shed and piling grain sacks on top of me. But then I saw that was impossible because leaning against the shed, watching the commotion, was the huge grain steward.

He looked around, and his eyebrows rose. "Yes?"

I put as cocky a grin as I could on my face. "Good day, sir."

"Were you supposed to be up those stairs, young feller?"

"No."

The man eyed me for a moment, and then broke into a grin of his own. "I remember you. You came with Charlie Judde to pick up the grain tax a week or two ago."

I kept on grinning. "That's right, sir."

"No."

"How's Charlie doing?"

"Fine, sir."

He listened to the shouting that echoed through the courtyard. Voices angrily called my name. "Just between you and me," he said frankly, "I'll be glad when all you little scamps get out of here."

I didn't reply, but kept well out of sight in the shadows of the staircase.

"It's bad enough with all the knights and squires dashing around like chickens with their heads cut off," he continued. "Add 40 kids, and you've got a madhouse. I'll bet a lot of these boys never saw the inside of a castle before. They don't know how to behave."

My cue. I was ready for it.

"Sir, is it true that there's an escape tunnel under the moat?"

"Sure."

"Could I"—my heart was beating against my back teeth—"see it?"

He shrugged. "Sure. I can't let you go down it, but there's the door, right there. Here, I'll go open it for you."

As we crossed the open courtyard, I stayed ahead of him on the wall side. I have never been so frightened in my life.

"And the escape route's still open?" I asked. "Nothing has blocked it?"

"Nope. I cleaned it out myself a month ago. The baron wanted it in working order again for some reason."

The whole time he slowly opened it I was in agony, but managed to stand there calmly. "There, take a look," he said. "You won't see anything. It's a black hole until you get under the moat. But it's clean as a whistle. I made sure of that. Then you pop out into the meadow like a rabbit out of— Hey! Come back here!"

Into the blackness I dived. My right knee smashed against something hard, and then it felt warm with blood. Down I scrambled, discovering that the steps were huge, but I continued to lunge forward, feeling frantically with my hands and my feet. Down, down, down.

Up behind me I heard a hollow shouting. When I hit a level place, I forced myself to run, tripping in the absolute blackness, getting to my feet and racing again, my hands outstretched like the feelers of some frantic insect.

At last I saw the beautiful pale gleam of daylight. Rushing toward it, I discovered that it came from a chink in a flat stone overhead. I pushed upward on it, harder and harder. Finally it broke free, and I scrambled out into the brilliant sunshine. Without stopping, I dived for cover in some high weeds.

And then I heard a horrible rattling and creaking. When I whirled around, I saw the castle drawbridge lowering. I could hear the squealing of horses, but thankfully, no sound of a dog.

But the next instant I thought of something that made me jump to my feet again and break into a dead run. They may have let Garth down the tunnel, and if so, he was due to pop his head out of the same hole I'd just come through. Too late to go back and close the stone trapdoor. Instead, I burst over a hillock and down into some trees. I ached to be able to hide in the heavy brush, but I knew Garth would find me there. So I kept running.

As I spotted a stream, I remembered an old trick. After wading out into the water, I splashed downstream for several yards before heading for shore again.

Seconds later I heard the horses, and this time a dog raced with them, barking madly. I followed the stream, crossing it again and again, and then dodging through a heavy stand of trees. Once in a while I would pause and listen.

Suddenly I knew, by the change in sound, that the horses were coming closer.

CHAPTER 22

My knees weak with fear, I waded out into the stream again, the water getting deeper and deeper. Finally I found myself among tall cattail reeds.

Beyond a thin stand of trees I could hear the thunder of horses, punctuated by the high barking of Garth.

Slowly I settled myself into the water, holding my backpack above me to protect it, trying not to bend the reeds as I did so. The clammy water rose to my neck and then around my ears, and I poised myself there, a weary blackbird, wounded by fear and longing for life and safety.

The horses approached, paused, and then passed on.

It was late afternoon by the time I made it to the meadow. I was starving. When I saw no horses on the horizon, I ran miles at a time without stopping, pacing myself, dodging through wheat fields and groves, throwing myself flat on my face if I saw anyone.

Alinor still waited in the meadow for me. She spotted me before I saw her, and she came running. "Denis, Denis," she repeated over and over, her face extremely white. Then she grabbed me by the shoulders and shook me with happiness.

"There's no time to talk, Alli. I didn't have time to flash quickly. But I'm in trouble. Get me into the castle. The baron and a bunch of his knights are after me. And that black hunting dog of his."

"Why? What happened?"

"Just get me into that castle, and get that drawbridge up. I won't feel safe until then," I panted, and with a look backward I took off running.

"Wait," she called. "Wait!"

When I paused, she put her fingers to her lips and whistled loudly. From across the meadow came an answering squeal, and the giant white horse thundered toward us.

My jaw slack, I watched him while Alinor grinned at me. "Angel," she said.

"Angel?"

"My horse. I figured that if I had to live in town she had to, too. Sir Robert owns this field, and when I came here he brought her from the castle."

The moment Angel reached us, Alli caught her mane and leaped on her back, sidesaddle because of her dress. "Come on. Here." She gave me her hand, and after much scrambling, I finally found myself perched behind her on the giant haunches of the mare.

As we pounded out of the meadow, I glanced sideways at the two farm buildings. The rope still stretched between them, and there, still hanging from it, was the Y-shaped twig. Suddenly I felt very much like that twig.

We galloped along the road that ascended to the castle while I kept glancing back over my shoulder. When we were still a quarter of a mile from the castle, I saw my pursuers closing in on us.

"Alli! Hurry! There they are!"

She glanced over her shoulder. "There's a dog with them."

"That'll be Garth. Come on! Hurry!"

"There's no need."

"Trust me, Alli. They want my blood. I've got a paper with me that'll incriminate them."

"We're OK, Denis."

My heart went to my throat. "I'm jumping off. You just don't understand. I've got to get to the king. I'll run ahead. They won't bother you if they see you alone."

"Denis." Her voice was cool. "Don't worry. Grandpa knows you're in trouble. As soon as I saw your flash, I signaled the castle. I'd arranged with the watchman to keep an eye on the town in case I needed to alert them. The watchman sent Sir Robert down, and I told him what I knew—that you'd gone to the baron's castle for the trials and that you'd signaled. So don't worry."

The baron and his knights were much closer now. I could hear Garth's baying.

"Denis, be calm. Look, up on the castle walls."

I did. And looked again. The walls were alive with soldiers, each armed with either a crossbow or a longbow. Alinor raised her hand, and I realized that she was catching the light of the late-afternoon sun and signaling the soldiers with her mirror. I saw two or three rapid flashes in return.

And suddenly I felt very calm. "Alinor, you are wonderful."

She half turned and I saw her smile. "So are you."

I opened my mouth to say something else, but decided not to. Instead I glanced back at the baron and his knights. They too had noticed the soldiers on the walls. Now riding quite slowly, they halted just before they got within crossbow range. Garth bounded on ahead, barking at us, but the baron roared him back.

And then the baron and his men wheeled their horses and started toward town.

★ ★ ★ ★

"Wait a minute," I said, facing Alinor and looking her squarely in the eyes. We were standing in the purple twilight of the courtyard. "You are refusing to let me see His Majesty?"

"Yes," she replied calmly.

"But he needs to see this oath."

"You can talk to him later."

"Alli, use your head. The baron is somewhere out there plotting a rebellion. Who knows? He may even be turning the townspeople against us right now."

"Grandpa doesn't think it will be that easy," she said thoughtfully. "Anyway, you can see him in three hours. He knows you're here."

"Does he know *why* I'm here?"

"He suspects."

"And he doesn't want to see me?"

"No. Not now. In fact, he suggested that you do something else first."

"What?"

"Come with me to the Great Hall, and I'll show you."

"The book of the chronicles?" I asked.

She grinned at me. "You guessed right."

She brought me a bowl of raisins and half a loaf of bread. Next she placed the huge book on the table and adjusted a candlestick holder so its light shone over my shoulder. "Now just read. And when you're all done, come to my room and get me. Then we'll go see Grandpa."

CHAPTER 23

The chronicles weren't easy to read. Bitter memories filled me as I thought of my dying parents. But suddenly I discovered that the king himself had written the book. The pen was his, and his hand had formed the words. And somehow, when I realized that, it made me lose a lot of the bitterness.

And what was even more amazing was that the king's handwriting was almost exactly like my own. He formed the capital letters exactly the way I did, making the same curls here, the same slant for the italics, the same dot for the *i*. It puzzled me, because I'd seen enough books to know that handwriting styles were quite different. That the king and I could write so similarly made me wonder.

However, I had no time to think of that. Because as I read, I was learning that this man, my king, understood his people far more than I had thought he did. I passed the place where I'd read to before, about the start of the plague. The further I got into the book, the more gripping it was. And then I came to where he told how hard it was for him to give the command for the soldiers to separate families. "It fills me with great bitterness," he wrote, "and my people hate me for it, but the dreadful truth about this plague is that it can be transferred from the dead to the living. By separating the living from the dead, I save the living."

At this part I began to cry quietly, until in horror I saw that my tears were smearing the ink. Finally I reached the end of the story. Many blank pages still remained in the book. I set it back on the reading stand and went upstairs to Alinor's room.

"I'm done," I said quietly.

She looked at me in silence, then asked, "Do you feel better?"

I took a shuddery breath. "Yeah."

"You've been crying."

"Yeah," I said again.

"I'm sorry."

"Don't be. No need to be."

"Grandpa's gone through some hard times."

"Yeah, I guess I can understand that now."

"He's had some rotten choices to make," she said softly. "It seems as though most of the choices he's faced with are all bad, though some are worse than others. Sometimes he has to decide which choice will hurt the least amount of people and save the most."

Suddenly I slumped on my knees before her, my right hand covering my tear-filled eyes. "I'm sorry, I'm sorry," I said as sobs shook me.

"That's OK." And she put her cool fingers on my shoulder.

"I've been a total idiot," I sobbed. "I've been nothing but a dirty, foul, traitorous dog."

"Denis, that's in the past. You meant well. Remember

Grandpa's rule? 'Treat people gently, as though they mean well.' That's how Grandpa can stay so calm when people are so angry at him. He knows that most of them mean well. They don't know any better. Grandpa realizes that when many of the well-meaning ones see the reasons behind the things he did, they'll respond to his love and change—just as you've changed."

Tears still tracking down my cheeks, I looked up at her. "Do you think I've changed?"

"Yes. You're not as . . . tough as you used to be. You always had this shell around you, even from the first, and nobody could ever get through it. Now I think it's gone."

★ ★ ★ ★

Alinor led me to the king's chambers, but to her surprise, he wasn't there. "He must have gone down to the Great Hall," she said.

When we entered the hall, we saw a hooded figure seated on the couch, his back to us, staring into the fire.

I stopped in the doorway, trembling, and whispered, "Alinor . . ."

She stopped and looked at me. "What's wrong?"

"Who is that on the couch?"

"Grandpa."

"I remember that hood from somewhere."

She stared at it. "That's a favorite robe of his. It's getting too old to wear in public, but—"

"The scholar!" I whispered.

She whirled on me with an amazed smile. "I wonder! Let's ask him." Grabbing my hand, she pulled me across the floor and around one end of the couch. "Grandpa, here's Denis."

The king looked up and smiled. And I knew. "Hello, Denis. Remember this robe?"

I nodded.

"It was I who taught you. I wanted to share what I knew with the village, so I disguised myself every Thursday and came down to town to be a teacher." He smiled. "When I met you on the road with those other boys, and you showed me your book, I didn't recognize you at first. But then it dawned on me who you were. But I was afraid to tell you who I was, because from what you told me when you studied with me, I knew you felt bad about some of the things I had to do."

I knelt before him.

"That floor's pretty cold," he said. "Here, come sit beside me. Alinor, you sit on the other side. That's right. There we go. Now we're comfortable."

And as I felt his royal arm across my shoulders, suddenly Denis Anwyck, the world's biggest crybaby, buried his face in that massive royal chest and sobbed like a long-lost son who'd finally found his father. And then, with his strong arm around me, I went safely and soundly to sleep.

CHAPTER 24

The next morning the king, Alinor, and I ascended to the highest watch turret.

"Now, Denis," His Majesty said, "you had something you wished to tell me."

"Yes, Sire."

I told him everything I knew. It was hard at first—because I still had traces of the old suspicion and fear—but it got easier and easier. When I sobbed out my treason, Alinor weeping in sympathy with me, he told me he forgave me.

Then I gave him the baron's oath. He took it in his hands. "Mordred, Mordred," he repeated softly.

I watched his eyes. He didn't even glance at the oath itself. Instead he studied the bottom of the page where the knights had made their marks.

"These are good men," he said sadly.

For a while he was silent, staring off in the distance. Then he turned to me and began asking me many rapid and detailed questions about the baron's castle. When I mentioned that the grain shed boards were used for the cudgel trials, he looked very alert.

"That reminds me. Can you tell me exactly what happened when you helped bring the grain tax? I've been wondering about that. I thought Mordred was going to refuse to pay it."

I told him what I could remember, ending with the baron's insistence that we leave the boards off the top so the oriental grain would cure properly.

"That wasn't grain," the king interrupted. "The cook found that out when he tried to make breakfast cereal with it this morning. What it is we're not quite certain, but it's not good to eat."

"Grandpa!" Alinor exclaimed. "Look!"

A brilliant orange ball of fire had blossomed far away on the western horizon. It seemed to be spewing upward from the baron's castle.

"What is it?" I asked. "What does it mean?"

A roar like a thunderclap thumped our eardrums. From the fields below us we could hear the screams of frightened horses. Farmers shouted questions to one another.

The king's face was grave. "Gunpowder. I should have suspected it. But why there? Why not here?"

"Gunpowder, Sire?" I asked blankly.

"Gunpowder is a hellish invention from Asia. It is a powerful powder that will explode if a flame touches it."

"Your Majesty," I said quickly. "Shouldn't we fortify the castle? Won't the baron think we had something to do with that fire?"

"Yes, we must fortify. Alinor, please find Sir Robert and send him to me. Denis, please go down to the courtyard and examine it carefully, especially around the grain shed."

Downstairs, I ran across the great open space toward the grain storage shed that still lay wide open to the sun.

I stopped in my tracks.

On the stone pavement, 30 feet from the shed, lay something that turned my heart to ice. It was a crossbow arrow, feathered at one end and covered with a black tarry substance at the other. Part of the arrow shaft was charred.

"A fire arrow," I whispered, feeling the pitch. It was slightly warm.

Suddenly I heard a whizzing high above me. A thunk and then a clattering sound, over by the grain shed. I stared in horror. A fire arrow had landed against a wooden post just 10 feet from the shed, and the flaming pitch flickered against the wood.

And suddenly I understood.

"Crossbow!" I screamed, leaping at the arrow and extinguishing it. "Archers outside the walls! They're shooting fire arrows!"

Even as I called the warning, I could hear the shouting of sentries up on the walls. They'd spotted the arrow too. The clickety-click of winding crossbows sounded above me. Then silence—as they waited for another arrow so they could pinpoint the bowman's position.

I glanced quickly around. The boards that normally covered the shed were stacked neatly against the castle wall. But they were too heavy for a boy to lift high enough to cover the shed.

So instead I ran toward the shed and vaulted over on top of the grain sacks. It was the white ones I went for. Scrambling and sweating under the fearful sky, I hoisted and tugged until they were all together in one pile in a corner closest to the castle wall. And then I covered as much of them as I could with my body.

"Denis?" Alinor's face appeared over the wall of the shed. "What are you doing?"

"Alli, get some men to put the boards on this shed. There's gunpowder in these sacks!"

Her face disappeared, and I could hear her running across the courtyard.

Thunk. The bowman had fired again, and I glanced crazily around me and above me, trying to see where it had landed.

Instantly, from high atop the walls, I heard the twanging of the sentries' crossbow strings. "Where is he?" I heard someone shout.

"Watch carefully," another ordered.

Running feet echoed through the courtyard.

Suddenly a sizzling flame sputtered close to me, and I saw that an arrow had landed just outside the wall of the shed.

"Help!" I cried. "Somebody put it out!"

Suddenly one of the roof boards crashed into place above my head. Leaping off the white sacks, I glanced outside. Two servants were carrying another board toward me. "Get out of there, lad!" one of them shouted.

I scrambled out. "The gunpowder's in that corner!" I said, pointing, and they slid the wide board all the way to the rear to shield it.

Alinor suddenly appeared beside me, and together we raced back up to the watch turret next to the king's chambers. As we suspected, the king himself was there, alone, watching the countryside. On the horizon rose a towering cloud of heavy gray smoke.

He smiled when he saw me. "Good. You're safe."

"The shed's covered, Sire."

"My sentries tell me you protected the gunpowder with your body. That was brave of you." He turned back to the window. For several minutes we watched the blazing castle. Then suddenly the king said, "Look out there. I think I see someone riding along that country road."

I shaded my eyes. "That cloud of dust, Sire?"

"Yes. What do you see?"

"A horseman, Sire. On a brown horse . . . and it looks like he's riding bareback."

"Who is it?"

The rider had just topped a small rise, and I could see more clearly. "He's going awfully fast."

"He rides like a boy," the king observed.

"A boy, Sire?"

"A boy who knows horses—but who is too frightened to worry about pacing his mount."

As we spoke, the rider drew nearer and nearer. He certainly was not sparing the horse.

"I recognize that steed," the king said. "It's one of Mordred's best. But who's riding it?"

I squinted. "It looks like . . . I think it's Max!"

The king turned to me alertly. "Your young friend with the sword? The knight-in-training?"

"Yes, Sire. He and I went together to the trials at the baron's castle."

"Roger!" the king cried out sharply. A sentry on the wall below us turned his head upward. "Roger! There's a boy riding toward us from the west. Make sure he's protected."

"Yes, Sire," the sentry shouted, and began barking orders to the other soldiers on the walls.

"The sentries still haven't spotted the bowman outside the walls," the king murmured. "And he may have orders to shoot anyone suspected of defecting from Mordred's castle."

I glanced down at the wall below us and saw that now it was bristling with crossbowmen, weapons at the ready. We could see Max clearly, clutching the horse around its neck, the exhausted stallion laboring up the long approachway Alinor and I had ridden the day before.

"Sire," I said. "Look at Max's face. His clothing."

"That boy's been burned. Roger! Find the physician! Have him ready to meet the rider."

"Yes, Sire!"

"Now," the king sighed, "let's go down to meet him."

CHAPTER 25

When we reached the courtyard, a stablehand was already walking the riderless horse back and forth to cool him down safely.

Max lay on his back on a heap of straw beside one of the stables. A thin man with a short goatee beard—the physician, evidently—bent over him. And from the way Max twitched and twisted, I could see that the doctor was gently examining his burns.

"Max," I said as I knelt beside his head. "What happened?"

"Wait," the doctor cautioned. "Don't make him talk quite yet. He's probably in shock."

Max rolled his eyes up at me, staring at me for a few seconds as if he'd never seen me before. Then he blinked, and recognition flooded into his face. "Denis," he whispered. Then, remembering, he twisted away from me, raising one hand to ward off my blows.

"Max, be calm," I said cheerfully. "Nobody's going to hurt you. Forget what you did at the baron's castle. Don't try to talk."

Footsteps behind me told me that the king had approached. Max saw him and tried to turn over to his knees, but the doctor held him gently down.

"How is he doing?" the king asked in a gentle voice.

Suddenly Max shut his eyes tightly, and from their corners I could see beautiful crystal tears welling up.

"Max," I said. "Hey, Max, it's OK. You're safe now."

As he nodded several times I could see he was trying to keep from bursting into sobs.

"How is he, Doctor?" the king asked again.

"A couple of mild burns is all. What you see on his face and body is soot. A little of his hair caught on fire, but that'll grow back in no time."

Suddenly Max opened his eyes and spoke in a weak voice. "Your Majesty."

The doctor put a gentle finger over the boy's mouth, but Max jerked his head away and struggled to a sitting position. "Your Majesty, I must talk with you at once."

"Please lie down," protested the doctor.

"At once," Max repeated. "It's important."

The doctor glanced at the king, who stood looking down at Max. Then the king sat down beside us, cross-legged, on the stone pavement. "I'm ready to listen."

Max's face twisted as though he were going to cry again, but he set his chin, breathed deeply, and began. "Your Majesty, I must ask forgiveness of Denis first."

"Hey, Max, forget it," I said, motioning with my hand. "I forgive you. You're my brother, remember?"

His voice trembled. "When you escaped, Denis, the baron and a few knights rode after you. They got back late at night, and from our tents in the courtyard we could hear that they were angry that they hadn't caught you. Then this morning the baron called all the knights to a council meeting in the hall of the keep. The squires went with them. That left us boys alone."

A momentary smile quirked the corners of the king's mouth. "I think I see what's coming," he said.

"And one of the boys found a big barrel of pitch arrows," Max gulped, "and somebody else smuggled fire from the servants' kitchen. And we started lighting them and shooting them—with my crossbow."

"Uh-ohhhh," I murmured.

"We started aiming them straight up in the air. Some of them fell outside the castle."

"But then—" I started to say.

"But then it was my turn, and the one I shot landed in that grain shed. You know the shed I mean, Denis."

"Yeah. And then to your surprise, everything blew up."

He stared at me. "Did you know what was in that shed?"

"Not until somebody started launching fire arrows into here early this morning. It was those white grain sacks they were aiming for. That wasn't grain, Max. It was— What did you call it, Your Majesty?"

"Gunpowder," the king answered gravely. "Was anyone killed?"

"I don't know. I hope not. The courtyard was pretty empty. But the next thing I knew, I was flying through the air. I must have landed among the horses, because there was a lot of squealing and stamping. A brown horse was choking itself trying to escape from where it had been tied. I grabbed it by the halter and finally got it calmed down."

"Is that the one you rode here?" I asked.

"Yeah. Because all of a sudden I got this horrible feeling. I was the one who'd shot that arrow. And I knew the other kids would tell on me to the baron when he got back, just the way I did on you."

Max shivered. "I hate him," he said in a low voice. "What he was teaching us to do was to have total faith in just one person—him—and you'd get rewards if you squealed on somebody who was against him. Anybody. Even"—he gulped—"your brother."

The king nodded. "Mordred has always considered himself the most important person in his life."

"So when I got the horse calmed down, I looked around for a saddle but couldn't find one. Quite a few of the other kids got knocked out, and they were just waking up. Figuring it was now or never, I hopped on the horse, and off we went. For some reason they'd left the drawbridge down. Otherwise, I wouldn't have gotten out alive."

"Did anybody follow you?" the king asked.

"I don't think so. I didn't see any of the knights."

"Maybe they thought they were under attack," I suggested.

The king got to his feet. "Young man, I think your parents should know where you are. I'll send a messenger to the village." He turned to me. "And Denis, what about you? You're free to go with Max, of course."

I looked up into his eyes. "Do I have to, Sire?"

His face broke into the most radiant smile I have ever seen on anybody's face. "You wouldn't mind staying?"

"If you would honor me by letting me stay just a little while more?"

"My child, I will give you anything you really choose." Then he opened his arms to me.

And while Max turned decently away and began to watch the young milk cow chewing on the catapult ropes, the king's great arms wrapped around my shoulders. And to my great wonder, I heard him weep.

CHAPTER 26

From the journal of Denis Anwyck:
I have put three large logs on the fireplace here in the Great Hall. It's midnight. Alinor and His Majesty have gone to their chambers, but I'm too excited to sleep, so I guess I'll write about what happened today.

Today was Royal Day. It happens once a year. It's the day the king calls everyone to the main square in town and speaks to them from the balcony of the council house.

Royal Day didn't mean much to me before today. Max and I could never get close enough to understand what was going on. We'd listen for a few minutes, and then we'd sneak off through the crowd with some other kids and run laughing and screaming through the empty streets.

But today I myself was on the balcony.

★ ★ ★ ★

From the open doorway to the balcony, Alinor and I could hear the murmuring of thousands of people. "It's almost time, Sire," Sir Robert told the king, who was adjusting his crown.

I moved to where I could get a better view. Beyond the edge of the high balcony was a huge crowd that stretched all the way across the square and spilled into the streets beyond.

"Are you scared?" Alinor whispered to me.

"Yeah."

"It'll be OK."

"But will they be able to hear me?"

"You'll be fine, Denis," Sir Robert assured me. "You're above their heads, so there isn't anything to block the sound. The wooden shell above the balcony has been designed to amplify voices. Just remember to stand in the circle I drew for you. The resonance is best right there."

It had been Alinor's idea—sort of—and I happened to be watching the king's face when she mentioned it back in the Great Hall. "Grandpa," she said, "why don't you have Denis tell the people about the baron's plot?"

He glanced at her quickly, then stared into a high, vaulted corner of the hall, tasting her idea. "There might be something in that," he answered. "No, on second thought, we'll ask Denis to read his journal to them."

At this I entered the conversation.

"No," I gasped. "I mean, I'd rather not, Sire."

"Why not?" Alinor asked.

I flicked an annoyed glance at her, and then turned anxiously to the king. "What good would it do, Sire?"

"At this point in the nation's history it would do far more good than anything I could say," he replied slowly.

"But you're the king, and I'm just an orphan."

"That's what I mean. Rank or position won't then get in the way when you stand before them."

I broke out in a sweat. "No," I said over and over. "No. Please, no."

Alinor wasn't any help. "Grandpa's right, Denis. Just read them your book."

"Your Majesty," I said desperately, "there are a lot of things in that book I'm ashamed of. Most of it I don't believe anymore. As soon as I can find a sharp knife, I'm going to cut those pages out."

"No," the king replied instantly. "Denis, promise me you will not do that."

"But, Sire—"

"Never do that. Not even after you read them to the people from the balcony on Royal Day."

"But Sire," I protested again, "what good will it do for me to read all that to them?"

"Denis, your journal contains an honest record of how you struggled to understand me. And believe me, you aren't the only one who went through those struggles. As you read of your bitterness, the people will remember their own."

"But won't that cause them to rise up in anger and revolt? Won't that give the baron the opening he wants?"

"Mordred will not be with us on Royal Day. I invited him to come, but he refused. He said he needed to supervise the rebuilding of his castle wall."

The king finally persuaded me to read my journal to the people. "You may leave out anything personal," he said, "but if it has to do with your feelings about me, the people need to hear it."

The palms of my hands were sweaty. With one of them I pressed my journal to my chest. With the other I clutched the strap of my backpack. "Maybe I'd better leave this inside," I said, starting to remove the pack.

"No," said the king, "I'd rather you took it out with you." He smiled. "After all, I have to wear my crown—you might as well wear your backpack."

"It'll be like a uniform," Alinor explained. "It shows who you are and what you do."

"Ready, Sire?" Sir Robert asked.

The king took a great breath. "Give the signal."

Sir Robert stepped onto the balcony. Trumpets immediately sounded close at hand, a brilliant, high chanting that made my blood race.

Alinor gave me a push, and together the king and I stepped out onto the balcony before the acres and acres of upturned faces.

I don't know how I ever got through the next hour. There was a high buzzing in my head. My voice seemed squeakier than ever. I took my eyes off my handwriting only once, when I looked over the edge of the reading stand and straight into the eyes of Max. Somehow he had managed to push his way to the front. He told me later that I looked white as a raw pine board.

But I read to them. I read about my dying parents. I read about my fear that the king's soldiers would come again someday and lock me in a dungeon. I read about the rebellion inside me that made me decide to attend the baron's trials. I read about my horror on hearing the oath his knights had sworn.

And finally, I read about coming to the castle and the king putting his giant arm around my shoulder, and feeling so safe and secure at his side.

When I was done reading, not knowing what else to do, I closed my book, turned, and walked through the doorway behind me.

Alli was waiting for me. As soon as I entered the room she threw her arms around me and kissed me three times. "You were great, you were great!" she said again and again.

"Stop that," I protested, blushing. "Could anybody even hear me?"

"I did, back here behind you. The people loved you."

I looked at her warily. "How can you tell?"

"Because of the way they were all crying."

"Crying?"

"Didn't you hear them?"

"No," I said wonderingly.

While Alinor and I were talking, I sensed that something was happening outside beyond the balcony. We both stepped to the door and looked out.

There was a lot of shouting going on, but gradually a single phrase took shape. Each time it was repeated it grew stronger, until the whole square rang with it:

"Long live the king!"

"Long live the king!"

"Long live the king!"

"Denis," the king said, "I have a question for you."

He and Alinor and I were back in the Great Hall the evening of Royal Day, seated at one end of a giant banquet table having dinner. A huge candelabra on the table lit up His Majesty's face.

"Yes, Sire?"

He looked me in the eyes. "Would you ever like to be a knight someday?"

I met his gaze. "No, Sire."

"No?"

"I think knighthood is foolishness," I replied firmly.

His Majesty smiled. "I wasn't thinking of that kind of knighthood. I was thinking of the knighthood that serves without superiority and battles without blood."

I gazed at him doubtfully. "But are there such knights, Sire?"

"Of course," Alinor broke in. "Sir Robert."

I nodded. "That's right. I guess I never thought of him as—well—"

"As someone who could wield a sword?" the king asked.

"Well, yes."

The king chuckled. "Robert was one of my best fencers at one time. But now he's a diplomat. He fences with words rather than blades. His foil and scabbard are rusting on the wall in his chambers."

Rising to his feet, he began to pace the floor slowly. "The splendid thing about you, Denis, is that you're knighthood material. You have courage to act on what you think is right, even if people are against you. And that's the first and most important qualification for true knighthood."

"But I don't like to kill," I protested, and told him the story of the redwing blackbird. "Swords make me sick."

"I'm really sorry about that," he said solemnly.

I stared at him. "Sorry, Sire?"

"Because I bought you one."

He reached into a pocket of his robe and placed in my hand a narrow velvet bag, jet black in color, about a foot long. Something square and hard rested inside. I fumbled with the silken drawstring at one end, opened it, and withdrew a slender mahogany case.

"What is it, Sire?" I breathed.

"Open it."

When I moved a gold clasp on the side of the case, the case split slightly. I opened it, and there, lying on black velvet, was a beautiful pen with shaft of silver and point of gold.

"*En garde,* Squire Denis," the king said.